"Is everything all right?"

Nothing's all right.

Nemo dropped to a sitting position and leaned against Fisk's side, and he ran his hand over the dog's back.

"Fisk?" It was Lauren's voice. She was holding her baby, Bonita.

He sucked in deep breaths, digging his fingers into Nemo's fur. "I'm fine. How's, uh, how's she doing?"

Lauren pulled up a stool to sit beside him, the baby in her arms. "Do you think she's got a fever?"

Fisk placed a hand on Bonita's forehead. His heart constricted. How many times had he done the same with his own child?

"I think she'll be fine after some rest and fluids."

"Do you think so?"

"It's common for kids to have a little bit of a fever with a cold." His heart rate was slowing back down to normal.

She nodded and swayed with the baby. "How do you know about babies, anyway, being an army medic?"

"They train us for a little bit of everything."

He didn't mention the fact that he had a baby of his own. Used to, anyway.

Lee Tobin McClain is the *New York Times* bestselling author of emotional small-town romances featuring flawed characters who find healing through friendship, faith and family. Lee grew up in Ohio and now lives in Western Pennsylvania, where she enjoys hiking with her goofy goldendoodle, visiting writer friends and admiring her daughter's mastery of the latest TikTok dances. Learn more about her books at www.leetobinmcclain.com.

Books by Lee Tobin McClain

Love Inspired

K-9 Companions

Her Easter Prayer
The Veteran's Holiday Home
A Friend to Trust
A Companion for Christmas
A Companion for His Son
His Christmas Salvation

Rescue Haven

The Secret Christmas Child
Child on His Doorstep
Finding a Christmas Home

Redemption Ranch

The Soldier's Redemption
The Twins' Family Christmas
The Nanny's Secret Baby

Visit the Author Profile page at LoveInspired.com for more titles.

His Christmas Salvation

LEE TOBIN McCLAIN

LOVE INSPIRED
INSPIRATIONAL ROMANCE

LOVE INSPIRED®
INSPIRATIONAL ROMANCE

Recycling programs
for this product may
not exist in your area.

ISBN-13: 978-1-335-93684-4

His Christmas Salvation

Love Inspired
22 Adelaide St. West, 41st Floor
Toronto, Ontario M5H 4E3, Canada
www.LoveInspired.com

Printed in Lithuania

MIX
Paper | Supporting
responsible forestry
FSC® C021394

Remember ye not the former things,
neither consider the things of old. Behold,
I will do a new thing; now it shall spring forth;
shall ye not know it? I will even make a way
in the wilderness, and rivers in the desert.
—*Isaiah* 43:18–19

To Pauline and Larry, the real Nemo's parents

Chapter One

Only a guy with issues would hold full-length conversations with his dog.

Fisk Wilkins made no secret of it: he was a guy with issues. "I'm peopled out," he said to his service dog, Nemo. "How about you? Dogged out?"

They were in Fisk's truck, headed home from a busy Thanksgiving dinner that had included two of his brothers, their wives, and their growing number of kids and dogs.

Nemo, a stocky poodle mix, had nearly flunked out of service dog training, and he'd only belonged to Fisk for two months. But they were already bonded. The dog's dark, intelligent eyes and alert head-tilt gave the impression that he understood exactly what his new owner was saying.

Fisk steered his truck carefully through the snowy downtown of Holiday Point. When the lampposts flickered on—each decorated with an evergreen wreath, bright red bow and white lights—he groaned. "Christmas decorations already?"

Nemo barked, possibly reminding Fisk that Thanksgiving Day was high time for holiday decorating. The few family groups strolling through downtown looked pretty happy about the season, too, stopping to chat or point at the lit-up window displays.

Fisk wasn't looking forward to Christmas. He would be doing this holiday season sober for the first time in a while. It wasn't going to be easy.

He touched the cross around his neck, then one of the AA coins in the bin between the seats, then Nemo.

Nemo let out his distinctive, high-pitched yip, seeming to understand Fisk's concerns.

Excessive barking was the flaw that had led to Nemo's near flunkout. The dog couldn't shut up. Fisk had volunteered at the training center while waiting for his service dog to be assigned, and he'd offered to take Nemo despite his imperfections.

Since Fisk lived in the hilly woods outside the town of Holiday Point, with only one other house nearby, the noise wasn't a problem for him.

Better a barking dog than enemy fire, any day. He and his sole neighbor, a Vietnam veteran, agreed on that.

Halfway down the icy dirt road that led to his rented house and woodshop, he spotted a silver car, nose down the embankment. It didn't look serious, but he could see exhaust smoke, so the car was still running.

Must have just happened. He jammed his truck into Park and got out.

Nemo barked.

"Come on," Fisk said, and the dog jumped out. Together, they slipped and slid down the slope to the driver's-side door.

He used his glove to rub away the icy, snowy film that had formed on the window. He could barely see the driver in the deepening dusk—just a lot of blond hair, so probably a woman. He tried the door. Locked.

And she rightly wouldn't want to open the door to a

strange man on a deserted road. "Your window," he called, making a circling gesture.

She lowered the window a few inches.

"Are you okay?" he asked. He still couldn't see her clearly. "Turn the car off."

She did as he'd said, and then Fisk heard a sound from the back seat. A fussing noise, increasing in volume.

The blonde woman fumbled with a bag beside her and then turned toward the back seat.

The sound of a crying baby threw him into the past. He could almost feel the weight of his daughter in his arms, just as he'd felt it the many nights he'd walked the floor to soothe her.

He shoved history and emotion aside, his army medic training taking over. "Either of you need medical attention?" he asked the driver through a tight throat.

She turned back toward him. Only it wasn't just any driver.

It was his girlfriend, his baby's mother, looking out at him.

Except it couldn't be. She was dead.

He tried to keep looking at her, wanting to prove to himself that he was wrong, but his eyes went blurry. His breathing quickened, and then the baby cried again.

His legs gave out.

He sank down into the snow on his knees, heart racing, the roaring in his head drowning out the sound of her voice and the memories.

Lauren Kantz lowered her window and studied her would-be rescuer. "Hey. You okay?"

He was on his knees, his head bowed. Even with his heavy coat, she could see that his chest was heaving. Was this some elaborate ruse? A criminal playing her, trying to get her to open her car door so he could rob her? A tabloid reporter who'd somehow discovered her destination in the wilds of Western Pennsylvania?

His snow-covered dog nudged and pawed at him, its yappy, high-pitched bark at odds with its substantial size.

Concern overrode caution. After making sure Bonita was secure in her car seat with her pacifier still in her mouth, she opened her car door—carefully, lest she cause the vehicle to move farther into the snowbank. Cold wind rushed in, and she shivered. "Sir? Sir, are you all right?"

The man shook his head back and forth a few times and squared his shoulders. He ran a hand over his dog. It stopped barking, though it continued to nudge at him.

"You there?" Gramps's voice boomed out of her phone speaker on the car seat behind her. "Lauren? I'm coming out to find you."

"No, I'm fine, I'm almost there," she half yelled in the general direction of her phone as Bonita started to fuss again. "Wait a minute."

She fumbled through the diaper bag on her passenger seat and found one of the sippy cups she'd prepared earlier. Leaning into the back seat, she offered it to Bonita. "Look, honey. Juice!"

Bonita stopped crying immediately and gave Lauren a two-toothed grin, then grabbed the cup and started sucking at it.

Lauren picked up her phone. "Sorry, Gramps. I drove into a ditch just down the road from your house, and then this guy in a truck stopped. Now he's—" She checked out the car door. "He's sitting in the snow and his dog is kind of in his lap. He doesn't *seem* like a threat."

"Brownish, curly-haired dog that yips a lot?"

At that moment, the dog let out another excited-sounding bark.

"Did you hear that?" she asked.

"That's Nemo," Gramps said. "And his owner is Fisk, my neighbor. He's a good guy."

"Okay. I'll talk to him and be there in a bit. I'm fine, don't come out." Gramps was a strong, healthy man, but his arthritis kicked up in cold weather. He didn't need to be walking through snow and ice.

She ended the call and checked that Bonita was still content. Then she got out and knelt before Fisk. "Hey. I'm Mr. Tucker's granddaughter. Are you all right? Want me to call someone for you?"

"You look like…whoa. Never mind. I'm fine." He nudged the dog out of his lap, at which point Lauren noticed that the pup wore a service vest.

Curiosity and sympathy tugged at her. You didn't get a service dog because life was easy.

Then, when the man met her eyes, something else tugged at her.

Uh-oh.

Her therapist's words came back to her: *Watch out when you're drawn to someone you don't know well. You're codependent. You can't trust your feelings.*

Her feelings had led her into the awful situation she was now escaping.

"So you're Gramps Tucker's granddaughter? Visiting him for the holidays?" Fisk seemed to be trying to shake off his confusion, or attack, or whatever it was that had caused his collapse.

"Yep." She dialed back her concern and stood. "Can you get back into your truck okay, or should I call someone for you?"

"No. No, I'm fine." He got to his feet. "I can help you get your car out."

That sounded like too long a process, and he didn't seem capable of doing it. "That's okay. I'll handle it tomorrow. I just need to get about half a mile down the road to Gramps's place, and—"

"Come on, I'll drive you." His voice still sounded ragged.

Lauren's mind ping-ponged around the alternatives as the sound of Bonita's renewed cries rose from the back seat. Walk to Gramps's place through the snow, dragging a couple of suitcases and Bonita? Call a tow truck on Thanksgiving Day and wait here in the cold, with a crying baby? Call Gramps back and ask him to fire up his old car and come out to get them?

Or take a ride with Gramps's neighbor, this so-called good guy with the penetrating, compelling eyes?

Gramps had said the guy was safe. "Uh, thanks, a ride would be great, if you don't mind waiting a minute while I gather my things."

"Fine. Hand me whatever you need, I'll load it in the back."

She pulled out a suitcase and the diaper bag, then extracted Bonita and her car seat. Lauren holding the baby and Fisk carrying everything else, they scrambled up the snowy slope. A moment later they climbed into his warm truck. Lauren clambered into the back seat and started strapping in the car seat. She made soothing noises to Bonita, who was perched on the seat beside her and looking around with the curiosity of a healthy one-year-old.

As she lifted the baby into the car seat and strapped her in, she spoke to the man she'd just met. "I know it probably seems weird to use a car seat for such a short distance, but—"

"Use it," he snapped. Then he looked away and adjusted a dog seat clip around Nemo.

Why had the man gone cranky on her?

Regardless of the reason, she was glad he was safety-minded. She settled in beside Bonita, leaving the front seat for the panting service dog.

"Da! Da!" Bonita cried when she saw it.

That was their only conversation during the three-minute ride to Gramps's place. As soon as Fisk had unloaded the bags onto the porch, he lifted a hand. "I'm right next door if you need anything," he said, his tone suggesting that he hoped she wouldn't get in touch.

As she hugged her grandfather and brought in Bonita and her things, Lauren pondered her strange rescuer.

He'd definitely been helpful. He'd done her a kind deed. But he'd seemed put off by her at the same time. In particular, he'd seemed to get upset at her mention of the car seat.

Or maybe it had nothing to do with the car seat. Maybe he'd recognized her. Did he know about her past?

She suppressed the circling, cycling worries. She had no intention of seeing this man again. He'd simply provided assistance to a neighbor, as folks tended to do out here in the country.

He seemed troubled and maybe a little strange.

And extremely good-looking.

She scolded herself for the thought. Maybe she'd bake him some cookies in thanks, but she'd make sure to have Gramps deliver them.

She didn't need to look into those soulful eyes, not ever again.

The next morning, Fisk was in his woodshop by 6:00 a.m., working on a coffee table made from reclaimed wood. He ignored Nemo, who snoozed on a rug by the door. Ignored the phone that had already rung twice and the stacks of paperwork spilling off the metal desk in the corner.

Ignored mental images that had kept him awake for much of the night and invaded his dreams when he'd finally slept. The pretty woman holding a baby, snow swirling around her, had suddenly morphed into his late girlfriend, Di, with baby Scarlett.

To stop himself from spiraling into a bad mental state, he looked over at Nemo and snapped his fingers. The dog came to stand beside him, stretching and yawning, back end high and front end low. Then he shook himself, sat down and leaned against Fisk's leg.

Fisk rubbed the dog's ears and then returned to his work, focusing on the sweet smell of oak and the steady sound of the hand planer. He needed to get this project sanded and stained this morning so he could start on his next project... Exactly which one was due next, he couldn't remember for sure. He'd have to sort through his paperwork and figure out the priorities now that he'd gotten several new rush orders over the weekend.

The good people of Holiday Point had rallied around him when he'd started his woodworking business, flooding him with Christmas orders for the benches, coffee tables and stand-alone cabinets he specialized in. He was determined to fulfill every request. He needed to repair his reputation in this town and pay back those he owed money.

It was all part of making amends, step nine in the twelve steps of Alcoholics Anonymous. He busied his mind with reciting all the steps as he continued work on the cabinet. Soon he was lost in the swirling grain of the wood and the sound of the orbital sander.

Outside, the sun had risen now, casting bright light

through the windows. Last night's storm was past, and although the world outside sparkled white now, much of the snow would be melted by noon.

There was a pounding on the door of his shop, and Nemo barked, facing the door, ears alert.

Fisk frowned. Who would come all the way out here on icy roads? His brothers, maybe, and worry turned his stomach. Had something happened to Mom or Dad? He went to the door.

"Pounded on your house door but there was no answer." His neighbor, fondly known to all as Gramps Tucker, entered without being invited. "Told her you were probably out here."

The "her" in question stepped in but stopped just inside the door, snowsuit-clad baby in her arms. "Gramps said it would be okay, but I can see that you're busy. We can come back another time."

Busy didn't begin to cover it. Besides, he was always busy. He glanced back, once, at the coffee table he hoped to finish today, and then focused on his guests.

Gramps Tucker, certain of his welcome, had shucked his coat and hung it on a hook by the door. Now he stood stomping snow off his ancient boots. "Come on, Fisk always welcomes a neighbor," he said with gratifying assurance. "Especially one who comes bearing food."

"Of course. Can I take your coat?" He helped her out of it, working around the baby. To avoid the memories that aroused, he concentrated on his five senses.

That might be a mistake.

Lauren's hair smelled like roses and shone like gold. Her voice, as she spoke nonsense words to her baby, sounded low and soothing.

He'd run away last night after dropping her and the baby

off, not even saying hello to Gramps Tucker. He should have known the older man wouldn't accept that.

"Come to bring you some coffee cake and check on my commission," Gramps Tucker said. "Wouldn't mind a cup of coffee, if you've got one."

"Coffee I've got." Fisk led them over to the small seating area in front of his desk and then poured coffee from the drip pot he'd filled this morning. He doctored the older man's cup with creamer from the small fridge and then turned to Lauren. "How do you take it?"

"I'm fine… Oh, wait. Is that Hazelnut Crème?"

"It is. It's my weakness." Well, the least of them, but she didn't need to know that. He poured her a cup and added a substantial dollop of the creamer, then set it on the desk beside her.

The baby, freed from her snowsuit, looked around the shop, eyes wide. She had big dark eyes and there was a reddish tint to her hair, an unusual combination.

She didn't look a thing like Scarlett, he assured himself.

Lauren, now that she'd taken off her own coat, didn't look all that much like Di had looked, either. Whereas Di had been as thin as a model, Lauren had curves. She also wore no makeup. Didn't need it. Her lips and cheeks were naturally a pretty pink, her eyes a rich shade of green.

He focused on his neighbor. "You shouldn't have come out in the cold. I could have updated you by phone."

"Wanted to see for myself," he said.

"I've got a ways to go on it," Fisk told him. Gramps Tucker wanted a corner cabinet for a friend, and he seemed very anxious that it get done on time. "Don't worry, though, it'll get finished by Christmas."

The older man looked at the desk, piled high with paperwork. "Quite a mess you've got there."

"I know," Fisk said. "I need to do something about it."

The phone rang. Fisk ignored it.

"You gonna get that?"

"They'll leave a message," Fisk said. "If I answered the phone all day, I wouldn't have time to get my projects done."

"You need to hire some help," Gramps Tucker declared.

"I do," Fisk admitted, "but I don't have time to find someone—"

"I have just the person," Gramps said. He held out his hands toward his granddaughter as if he were presenting her on a stage. "Lauren, here, has business experience. She was an office manager back in Harrisburg, and she needs a job over the holidays, where she can be near her baby."

Fisk blinked and then looked at Lauren. Her expression was as startled as the one he was sure was on his own face. So this wasn't premeditated between the two of them.

"I'd like the chance to get to know my great-granddaughter," Gramps Tucker went on, seeming oblivious to Fisk's and Lauren's reactions. "But if Lauren finds work over in Uniontown, I know she won't let me look after Bonita. Won't want to be so far away from her. If she works here, she'll be just a stone's throw away, and can check on us anytime she wants to."

Lauren looked at Fisk, shaking her head. "I couldn't ask that of you," she said. "You weren't even looking for an employee, right?"

"No, I wasn't," he said slowly. But he knew he was in over his head. Having someone to help temporarily, just with the Christmas orders, would be a blessing.

On the other hand, he couldn't work with someone who looked so much like Di, and with a baby the same age as Scarlett had been when...

"I mean," she said, "I do need work, but do you have

the budget to pay me, even part-time? I know Gramps said you're just getting started."

Fisk tried to keep his insulted feeling from showing on his face. He knew he looked rough, but he was doing better than he'd ever expected when he'd started the business.

Continuing to do well, though, was dependent on getting these orders organized and completed in a timely way while attending to emails and calls and last-minute changes, things he hadn't really considered when he'd made the rash decision to open a woodworking business.

And making this business succeed was central to his new, sobriety-fueled life plan. "I can afford it."

She tilted her head to one side. The stormy look he'd seen in her eyes was fading, replaced by something bright and excited. She handed her baby to Gramps Tucker. "Let's talk about it," she said, standing. "Show me what needs to be done."

Twenty minutes later, he had a new assistant. A beautiful woman he needed to stay away from, with a baby who was going to be a constant reminder of the one he'd lost.

What had he done?

Chapter Two

On Monday afternoon, Lauren heard a deep, masculine chuckle and looked over at Fisk from the passenger seat of his truck.

They were headed home from a shopping jaunt that had been surprisingly fun. Now, her hands stilled on the bag of office supplies in her lap. "Are you laughing at me?"

"Sure am. I never saw anyone get so excited about a bunch of file folders and labels."

"Pens, too. Don't forget the multicolored felt tips."

After assessing Fisk's paperwork situation this morning, she'd decided not to try to put his business online. Too much startup time, and the internet was spotty out where Fisk and Gramps lived. So she'd suggested a trip to the local big-box store for supplies to create a reasonable, paper-based filing system.

She'd expected to go alone, but it turned out he needed some supplies, too. Either that, or he wanted to keep an eye on her business spending.

Living next door to her place of employment was a dream come true. She'd gone back over to Gramps's place at noon, played with Bonita and fixed lunch for the three of them. Both Gramps and Bonita seemed thrilled to settle down with a heap of picture books after lunch, erasing any guilt Lauren might have felt about heading off for an office-supply-related shopping jaunt for the afternoon.

Maybe this was going to work. Maybe she could parlay the holiday job into something longer-term, something that could provide for Bonita and keep her safe.

"You're looking at them like you'd look at a chocolate cake." Fisk was still smiling as he steered around a curve in the mountain road.

"It's the same way you looked at that wall of sandpaper and nails," she said. "Stuff was all the same to me, but you must've spent half an hour studying it."

"They'd gotten in a new grade of sandpaper," Fisk said. "1000-grit, superfine. Who wouldn't be excited?"

He glanced over, one eyebrow lifted, gray-blue eyes sparkling with laughter.

He looked way, way too appealing.

Abruptly, Fisk returned his attention to the road.

Had he noticed her admiring him? Lauren's face heated. Time for a change of subject. She focused on the multicolored small discs that were collected in his between-seats console. "Those are pretty. Are they foreign coins?" She knew Fisk had served overseas.

"You don't know what they are?"

She scooped up a couple of the coins and studied them. She couldn't find a country name, but there were several lines of text printed tiny on the backs. She held one up to the light, trying to read it.

"It's the Serenity Prayer," he said. "They're AA coins."

Lauren's fingers went limp and she dropped both coins, then bent to find them, hoping Fisk wouldn't see her reaction.

Oh no, oh no, oh no.

She'd been right to feel cautious about being drawn to him. She knew, now, why she found him so riveting.

She located the coins and placed them back on the dash. "How long ago did you quit drinking?" she asked, hoping her voice sounded normal. "Is each one for a year?"

Maybe it had been a long time ago. Maybe so far in the past that it barely mattered, and she could still work for him.

He blew out a humorless laugh. "Each one's for a month," he said. "I got sober almost one year ago."

"Oh." Her shoulders went limp. Forget about anything long-term, work-wise, with an alcoholic. They couldn't be trusted.

"You seem to have a reaction to that information," he said, his voice calm. "Care to share what it's about?"

She hesitated. She didn't want to reveal anything that would send him looking into her past. "I…well, I have a history."

"You drink now? Or you drank in the past?" They were reaching the residential area of Holiday Point now, small, neat frame houses with front porches. Most were already decorated for the holiday season.

"No! I don't drink." She never had. "I have…a couple of alcoholics in my past, so I know how much damage…" She trailed off and looked over at him, just in time to see a flash of what looked like pain cross his face.

She didn't want to hurt him. "I know how hard it is to quit," she amended.

It wasn't a sufficient explanation. But it would have to do. No way was she sharing the details of her past unhealthy relationships, especially with someone who… She sneaked another glance at him. Really, he was an alcoholic? Why hadn't Gramps shared that information with her? He knew what she'd been through.

Of course, to develop a drinking problem, Fisk had probably been through a lot, too. Evidence for that was Nemo, panting in the back seat of the truck.

Sympathy for the square-jawed man beside her rose at the same time that her inner warning bell rang.

She *did* know how hard it was to quit, because she'd talked to a few recovering alcoholics during her journey to heal. She'd watched her father come out of rehab, twice, and start drinking again within the month. Her husband hadn't admitted he had a drinking problem, but that was denial; she knew he was an alcoholic. She also knew that alcohol wasn't the reason for what her husband had done and couldn't justify it.

She was vulnerable to alcoholics. She lacked skill at discerning what a man was like, based on her own feelings. It was a flaw in her makeup. She came by it naturally.

As they passed through Holiday Point, she saw something going on at a big old building that she vaguely remembered from her summers with Gramps. It had once been a small-town department store, if she were remembering right. Now the old store's sign was gone, but the place was active. People had pulled trucks up to the side door and were carrying big boxes inside. "What's going on there?" she asked. "Didn't that store go out of business way back?"

"It's a vendors' market now," he explained. "They do a big business over Christmas. Must be getting the displays ready."

"Vendors of what?"

"Oh, antique signs, or handmade crafts, or yard decorations. Toys. A little bit of everything."

"Stop the truck," she ordered.

He slowed down and looked over at her. "Why?"

"Park it," she said, gesturing toward one of the diagonal

spaces that was still empty. "Come on, I'm your new office manager. You have to do as I say."

He lifted an eyebrow but followed her request. After he'd turned off the truck, he looked over at her. "What's this about?"

Why did he have to be so attractive? "You need to be here. Your business needs to be here."

"What do you mean?"

"You need to display your merch there. Maybe even set up a workbench and do some simple project as a demonstration, to get people's attention."

He laughed a little and shook his head. "You don't know how bad an idea that would be," he said. "Besides, I can't keep up with the orders I have."

"Only because it's the holidays, right? You need to prepare for leaner times."

His expression was still doubtful, and he wasn't making a move to get out of the truck.

She opened the door, climbed out and looked back at him. "I wasn't just an office manager," she said. "I helped with marketing, and I'm good at it. I want to earn my pay and help you improve your business. Come on, let's talk to the organizers."

"But you don't understand—"

He was just being a man. He didn't want to do it because it hadn't been his idea. Fine. She'd talk to them herself and get his business on the map of Holiday Point.

Fisk blew out a breath and climbed out of his truck. He let Nemo out, too, and adjusted the dog's service vest, giving himself a minute to calm down.

This wasn't a terrible situation, he reminded himself. More like embarrassing.

He caught up with Lauren in the first hallway of the vendors' market. The smell of Christmas was in the air—a mixture of pine boughs and candles and hot chocolate from the little café.

Lauren stopped in front of a vendor who was adjusting her display of crocheted stuffed animals and place mats and other pretty, colorful items Fisk couldn't imagine using. Within minutes, Lauren was talking to the woman about sales and the pricing of booths, learning that the most expensive spaces were the ones near the front, where the most people walked by, and near the back, where Santa visits took place.

Santa visits. Fisk's face heated just thinking about that.

He saw a couple of people he knew from church and was thankful they waved in a friendly way. A couple of other folks turned away or gave him dirty looks, perfectly justified. Not only was he a member of the notorious Wilkins family, but he'd done plenty of individual stupid stunts to earn the disgust of the townspeople.

Lauren was near the back of the building now, talking with James Ferrell, a local dad who ran the vendors' market. He seemed to have taken a break from pounding nails near the Santa throne. They were nodding, smiling, getting along fine.

And then James spotted Fisk. He stopped talking, and his head tilted to one side. "Fisk. Didn't expect to see you back here."

"He's the carpenter I was telling you about," she said.

"I see." The man stood and brushed off his hands on his work pants. "So you want to do what, now?"

Shame rushed in on Fisk. "It's a bad idea. Lauren. Come on, let's go."

"I think a display of an actual woodworker would be fun

for the kids, especially while they're waiting to visit Santa," she said. "It would really interest the parents, too."

James looked from Lauren to Fisk and back again. "It does seem like a good idea, but I can't let this man anywhere near the kids."

Shock crossed Lauren's face and she took a big step away from Fisk. "What did you do?" she asked him in a shaky voice.

He swallowed hard. "I was the notorious drunk Santa last year," he told her, and then turned to James. "I'd like to do something to make up for that. If providing a demonstration for free would help you out, let's get it scheduled. I can keep well away from the kids, but she's right, the parents might enjoy it."

Lauren's face was white and she wasn't saying anything. What was *that* about?

James nodded. "I'd heard you got sober," he said. "I'd like to give you a chance to make amends, but I'll have to talk to my board."

Fisk pulled out a business card and handed it to James. "Give me a call if you want to set something up," he said. "If you decide against it, no harm, no foul."

"Sounds good." James shook Fisk's hand. "Glad to see you're getting your life straightened out."

Fisk thanked the man, turned and started walking toward the exit, studying the half-completed displays around him. This actually wasn't a bad idea. Lauren was right: he needed to think about his business year-round rather than just panicking about all the Christmas orders.

He looked back to thank her, but she wasn't there. She must have stopped to talk to someone. She seemed pretty outgoing and social.

When he spotted her, though, she was sitting on a ply-wood box, staring in his direction, face still white.

He walked back toward her. "Are you okay?" he asked, wondering if she were feeling sick.

She didn't answer, at least not directly. Instead, she stared at him. "What happened last year? Why can't you be around kids?"

Again, that hot flash of shame. "Like I said, I arrived with alcohol on my breath." He paused and then corrected himself. "I was drunk. After a few kids talked to me, the families got wise to it and I was booted out." He looked at the tile floor. "I'll just be glad if they let me come back and make it up to them in some way. I wouldn't expect to work directly with the kids again."

"You didn't do anything inappropriate?"

He studied her. "Well, being a drunk Santa is pretty in-appropriate, but…" Suddenly he realized what she must be thinking. "I've never done anything to hurt kids, Lauren, if that's what you mean."

"You realize I'm going to check up on that."

He spread his hands. "If you need to do that, I under-stand. You won't find anything."

"I hope not." She rose and stalked toward the door.

Fisk followed, all the good cheer around him unable to lift the dark cloud that was descending.

He knew he'd made a lot of mistakes, and he was com-mitted to staying here in Holiday Point to make things right, or as right as they could be. But the fact that lovely Lau-ren could suspect him of doing something so horrendous as purposely hurting a child discouraged him. Would he ever get beyond his past mistakes?

He put a hand on Nemo's shaggy head and tried to ig-nore the gloom settling around his heart.

Chapter Three

Lauren wasn't sure how Gramps had talked her into having breakfast at the Point Diner. It probably had to do with her own guilt.

Yesterday, she'd felt such righteous indignation about Fisk's history of bad behavior around kids at last year's Santa event. She'd come home from their stop at the vendors' market and let Gramps know that the job wasn't panning out and that she was going to have to leave.

The thought of working with someone who could hurt kids was simply repugnant. True, he'd said he hadn't done that, but could she believe him? It was a risk—too huge a risk.

She hugged Bonita tight against her side as they walked into the diner. Immediately, the fragrance of bacon and coffee assailed her, along with the cheerful din of morning coffee drinkers.

A moment of wistfulness overcame her. She'd hoped to stay, hoped to have the kind of small-town friend groups that might meet for breakfast at a little diner.

But if it put Bonita at risk, then no way.

Fisk was an alcoholic. She needed to find out the truth about whether he'd mistreated kids. Until she did, even living next door to him was dangerous; working for him was out of the question.

"I should be home packing," she told Gramps as they waited to be seated. She bounced Bonita. For now, that was working to keep her content.

"This is my normal day for meeting my buddies here." He scanned the diner. "If you're going to be leaving, at least meet my friends."

He sounded gloomy and depressed, and she looked over at him, concerned.

He was still perusing the place, and suddenly, his face broke out in a big smile. What was going on?

"Come on, over here," he said, and led the way to a booth where three women sat. "Lauren, I'd like for you to meet Olivia and Kelly. They're both teachers here in town. And this is Jodi, who's married to Fisk's brother Cam."

Gramps's buddies were three young women?

"Come sit down." Kelly, whose baby bump made the booth a tight squeeze, patted the seat beside her. "I'm married to a Wilkins, too. Fisk's oldest brother, Alec."

"And I'm Olivia. Not a family member, but almost."

Lauren forced a smile. "It's nice to meet you all, but Bonita and I had better sit with Gramps. There's not room for all of us here."

Gramps held out his arms for Bonita. "You sit down," he said to Lauren. "I'm going to show off this little lady to my friends." He gestured toward a table of older gentlemen on the other side of the restaurant.

"But—"

He scooped Bonita into his arms. "Want to come with Gramps, sweetie?"

"Gah," Bonita said agreeably, cuddling against his broad chest.

Lauren's heart twisted with longing. She wanted Bonita

to have a male influence and a close relationship with her great-grandfather. That part of things was working so well.

"I fooled you," Gramps admitted to Lauren, now all smiles as he cuddled the baby. "I wanted you to meet these ladies. They can tell you everything you need to know about your new boss." With that, he turned and made his way across the restaurant with Bonita in his arms.

Lauren stared after him, amazed. What a schemer! She'd sit with these ladies for a few minutes because it would be rude not to, but come on—of course, Fisk's sisters-in-law would try to paint him in a positive light.

Realizing they were all looking at her, Lauren slid into the booth beside Kelly.

"And they say women are manipulative," Jodi said, chuckling. "Your grandpa is a sweetheart, but he just pulled a number on you."

"He definitely did."

The waitress, whose name turned out to be Zoey, came over and took their orders. She seemed to be a good friend of these ladies, too. Was she also married to some other brother of Fisk?

After Zoey left, the other three got down to the business that Gramps had apparently prearranged with them. They raved over her cute baby, told her about their own kids and sang the praises of Holiday Point as a great place for a family.

"The elementary school is terrific," Olivia said, then looked over at Kelly and giggled. "Of course, we're biased. We both teach there."

"Don't you have to work today?" Lauren asked.

"Late start because the roads up in the mountains are icy. The rural kids' buses need extra time in this weather." Kelly fist-bumped Olivia. "We are *not* complaining. We love having the chance to hang out a little before class."

"And I love the chance to get out of the house," Jodi said. She turned to Lauren. "I have three little ones and I normally work at home, but my husband, Cam, agreed to stay with the boys this morning so I could come in and visit."

"He wanted you to defend his brother to me," Lauren said flatly. "That's why you're all here, I get that. But it's not going to work."

Their friendly faces fell.

"For sure, that's what your grandpa was shooting for," Olivia admitted. "But we would have wanted to welcome you to town, anyway."

The others nodded agreement. "Holiday Point is friendly, not cliquish," Kelly said.

Zoey came over with the coffeepot and filled everyone's cups, assuring them that their breakfasts would be right out.

"So," Kelly said when they were all sipping coffee, "Fisk. What do you want to know about him?"

"I *don't* want to know anything," Lauren said. She knew she was being unfriendly, and she didn't like herself for it. But she wasn't going to get sucked into female pressure. She had to do the right thing for Bonita.

She looked across the restaurant to check on her. Gramps had the baby on his lap and was holding court while a couple of locals stood by the table, smiling and admiring her.

"Your kiddo's fine," Olivia said. "And look, maybe you don't want to know anything about Fisk, but your grandfather said that you're going to quit working for him after one day and that you're planning to move away. You need to know the truth before you take those steps."

"I've known the Wilkins family forever," Kelly said, taking up the story, "and they've definitely had troubles. The parents still do. But Alec, my husband, has been able to overcome that and he's a wonderful man."

Nice for you, Lauren wanted to say, and she wanted to say it in a sarcastic voice. She pressed her lips together.

"Cam, too," Jodi said. "He's had to do some work to overcome his temper, but he's done that and continues to work on himself. He's worth the risk I was so scared to take."

"It's great you all have happy lives with Fisk's brothers," Lauren said. "But I'm not looking to marry the man. I just want to get away from someone who has an alcohol problem and very possibly mistreats kids."

"Mistreats *kids*?" Kelly's voice rose to a squeak. "That's not something Fisk would do. Not *ever*."

The others nodded vigorous agreement.

Lauren's stomach churned. How was she going to deal with this cheerleading squad for a man who kept messing up? She thought of her ex's sister, who'd been so vehement that he was a great guy. So had his mother. Wrong, all wrong.

"Sausage-egg-cheese sandwiches for the teachers," Zoey sang out, putting plates in front of Olivia and Kelly. "Jodi, here's your omelet. And Lauren, two eggs over easy and wheat toast. I brought it dry, but here's some butter and jelly." She placed a small bowl containing individual servings of each in front of Lauren's steaming plate.

The food did smell good, and Lauren took a couple of bites, then put down her fork. "Fisk and I went to the vendors' market yesterday," she said. "I was thinking he could do a woodworking display."

"What a great idea," Jodi said warmly.

But Olivia and Kelly looked at each other. "He showed his face there?" Olivia asked.

"He didn't want to," Lauren said, "but not knowing the story, I kind of insisted on it as his new office manager. It didn't go well."

"Oh no," Kelly said. "They weren't receptive?"

"Actually, the man we spoke with said he'd consider it," Lauren admitted. "But he also talked about Fisk being a drunk Santa. And he said Fisk couldn't be around kids. Which says to me that he's dangerous to them, maybe even has a history of some kind of criminal behavior."

"No way!" Olivia said. "He's not dangerous. He *was* intoxicated and he definitely botched the Santa job, but he's moved beyond that now." She took a big bite of her breakfast sandwich.

"And he didn't do any harm to kids, then or ever." Kelly wiped her hands. "He's very gentle with kids. I'd trust him around my daughter anytime."

"His struggles were more with judgmental adults," Olivia added.

Lauren blew out a breath. Could three nice women be entirely wrong? "Maybe I'm being judgmental myself," she said. "I'm just very cautious where Bonita is concerned, because of…well, because of something that happened."

The other women looked sympathetic. "I get that," Jodi said. "I had some history that made me super cautious around Cam. But I'm so glad I overcame it."

The other two nodded. "Same," Olivia said. "In fact…" She studied Lauren. "I'd like to see Fisk meet someone nice and settle down. Are you single?"

Lauren nearly choked on her toast. She waved her hand, coughing. "No. No way. I don't date."

"Yeah, I said that, too," Kelly said. She checked the time on her phone. "Oh, man, we'd better get over to the school. So nice to meet you, Lauren. I hope you'll think about what we've said."

"Of course, nice to meet you guys, too," Lauren said

faintly as the two teachers gathered their things, put money on the table and rushed out.

Jodi remained. "I'm sorry we triple-teamed you," she said. "It's just that Fisk is a good guy at heart. We all want him to stay sober and get on his feet. I know he's overwhelmed with this new business he's starting, and I wish we could help, but Cam and I have our hands full."

"Thanks. I do appreciate your taking the time with me. I'll give it some thought." Lauren looked over at Gramps, still holding court with Bonita on his lap. "I know he wants us to stay, and if I do, I need work. I guess I just freaked out with what I heard."

"That's understandable." Jodi's phone buzzed, and she looked at it and started to gather her things. "Duty calls. But if you ever want to talk or get together, I can make it happen. We all can, but I'm sure the three of us together can be a bit much."

That was an understatement, Lauren thought as she picked up her own things more slowly and headed toward Gramps's table.

The truth was, it would be great to have a resting place here, at least for a while. Gramps needed her, and it was mutually beneficial, since Holiday Point was remote enough from Harrisburg that they could be shielded from all that had happened.

If she were to stay, she'd need a job. And she *did* enjoy helping keep a business organized. Her fingers itched to start putting those office supplies to work.

The thought of seeing Fisk again made her heart beat a little faster, too, but no way was she going to pay attention to that.

She'd give the job with Fisk a try, but she'd work hard to keep her distance.

* * *

Lauren's presence at Fisk's desk, even all the way across the woodworking studio, kept distracting him.

It was Thursday morning, and Fisk was thankful that Lauren was here. After she'd worked all day yesterday, his desktop was actually visible, the paperwork in organized stacks. More importantly, he had a priority list of what to work on, based on phone calls she'd been making and emails she'd sent.

Most of his customers were fine with a slight delay. It helped that she introduced herself as his office manager and took a warm but businesslike tone on her calls. She was on the phone now, and he found he enjoyed the musical sound of her voice.

He reached down to rub Nemo's head and then focused on the bench in front of him, fitting the decorative legs to the smooth wooden top.

Lauren didn't trust him, he could tell. Not completely. But now at least, she no longer seemed to suspect him of being some horrible criminal and a danger to children. The very idea of that shocked him. It was ridiculous. The Wilkins family was known for getting in trouble, sure, but they specialized in misdemeanors, not felonies.

The tone of Lauren's voice changed, and Fisk realized he'd been listening to its low murmur in the background rather than turning on the music.

"Oh no, I was afraid of that," she was saying. "It's probably not a big deal, but I'll come home and check on her."

Fisk looked up in time to see her bite her lip. Then she stood. "I need to go check on Bonita," she said. "Gramps says she's congested and fussy."

"Do you want me to come?"

She looked at him like he'd grown horns. "No! No, I mean, why would you come?"

He held up his hands like stop signs and stepped back. "It's just, I was a medic in the army."

"Oh, right. Um…"

"If you want to bring her over here so you can keep an eye on her, that's fine. That was part of our agreement. And then, if you want me to take a look, I can."

She nodded doubtfully, shrugged into her jacket and headed across the snowy yard between his place and her grandfather's.

He sighed and got back to work, attaching the arms of the decorative bench. Soon, it would be ready for the stain and glossy varnish this particular customer had decided on.

He wasn't going to win everyone over, and that was okay. His AA sponsor had discussed it with him. Some people were easy forgivers, some were more difficult, and some never forgave at all. You had no control over that; you only had control of your own behavior. Beyond that, you had to turn it over to God.

He set the bench on the sheet-covered area where he did the staining and painting, then started planning out the next project on the list, a small curio cabinet.

When Lauren came back in, he deliberately didn't pay attention. She was the type who you had to let come to you; she didn't like being approached or overwhelmed, especially by someone she was already wary of. More like a cat than a dog, he thought, as Nemo returned from greeting her and settled by Fisk's side.

What had happened to her to make her that way?

He tore his eyes away from the tender sight of her settling the baby into a warm corner beside her desk. He focused on penciling in the necessary lines and circles on the light-colored beechwood.

When he turned on the jigsaw, he winced and looked over toward Lauren, worried he'd awakened the baby. Lauren smiled reassuringly and tilted her head onto prayer hands, the universal sign for "sleep."

He went back to work. This was nice. He could focus on his carpentry, and he appreciated the companionship in his shop.

After a while, he heard something discordant. The sound got louder, and his low-key irritation shifted into concern. That baby sounded sick.

His baby. Scarlett.

Everything in him lit up with hope and joy. She was here. She wasn't gone, she just had a cold. He could get to her, help her, soothe her hurts. He could hold her in his arms. He could—

As he started to stand, something pressed against his leg. He reached down and felt soft fur.

Nemo.

With his hand on the dog's shaggy head, his surroundings came into focus. He realized where he was.

Not in Baltimore with Di and Scarlett.

He was in Holiday Point with Lauren and her baby. Her baby, not his. Scarlett was gone.

He sank back down, his heart breaking all over again.

Nemo jumped his front paws to rest on Fisk's thigh and nudged his head under Fisk's hand.

"Sorry she's crying," came a woman's voice. "Are you okay?"

The words banged against each other in his head, making no sense.

"Fisk. Hey. Is everything all right?"

Nothing's all right.

Nemo dropped to a sitting position and leaned against Fisk's side, and he ran his hand over the dog's back. He looked down. Dark, concerned eyes watched him steadily.

"Fisk?" It was Lauren's voice. She was holding her baby, Bonita. "What's going on?"

He sucked in deep breaths, digging his fingers into Nemo's fur. *Focus. Answer.* "Nothing. I'm fine. How's, uh, how's she doing?"

Lauren pulled up a stool to sit beside him, the baby in her arms. "Do you think she's got a fever? I couldn't find a thermometer at Gramps's place. I know I packed ours, but I can't find it either."

Fisk placed a hand on Bonita's forehead. His heart constricted. How many times had he done the same with his own child?

"She's got a fever, doesn't she? I should take her to the clinic."

Fisk was coming back to himself, enough that he could study the baby. Her face wrinkled into a frown, and she cried just a little, in a low-energy way. But her pulse was steady, and there was a slight fever at most. He asked Lauren a couple of questions about her night and her morning. "She's warm, but not burning up," he said. "I think she'll be fine after some rest and fluids."

"Do you think so? I always worry."

"It's common for kids to have a little bit of a fever with a cold. Let's keep a close eye on her and we'll see how she's feeling later." His heart rate was slowing back down to normal.

She nodded and swayed with the baby, calming her. "How do you know about babies, anyway, being an army medic? I wouldn't think you'd have learned about pediatric medicine."

Fisk didn't want to give the real answer. "They train us for a little bit of everything. If we're in a town or village and a child needs medical support, we have to respond."

He didn't mention the fact that he had a baby of his own. Used to, anyway. "I still have my medical bag. Keep it in my truck for emergencies. I can grab it and look into her ears if you want. Sometimes, an ear infection causes these symptoms." That was something he knew as a father, not as a trained medic. It was also something concrete to do, which would help him stay in the present instead of drowning in the past. He'd learned that through past experience with this kind of episode.

"No, it's okay," she said, standing. "If she gets worse, maybe, but for now, you need to get back to work. You have orders to fill."

"I have time—"

"No, you don't. Get back to work." She turned and headed back toward the office area.

"Yes, ma'am." As he watched her go, he felt the corners of his mouth lifting into a smile. He'd never been the best at staying on track. Needed someone to keep him focused, and Lauren seemed tailor-made for the role.

Don't get any ideas about her, he warned himself. *You're a mess, and you don't deserve love and a family.*

A loud knocking on the shop door provided a distraction. He started to stand, but Lauren waved him back. "I'll take care of it," she said, heading to the door with a sleepy-looking Bonita on her hip. "You work."

When she opened the door, though, it was harder to stay focused, because his most difficult customer walked in. "I came to check on my project," Mrs. Wittinger said sharply.

"Now I see why there's going to be a delay. You're playing house in here."

Not wanting Lauren to have to deal with the woman alone, Fisk stood and walked over. "I'm sorry, Mrs. Wittinger. I'll prioritize it." Who needed sleep? He'd work on it all night. Mrs. Wittinger was influential in town and at church, and he didn't want to damage the slight good reputation he'd been building.

Lauren had walked back over toward the desk while he'd been speaking, and now, she returned with a clipboard. "Actually," she said to Mrs. Wittinger, "you've been moved to the bottom of his list."

Mrs. Wittinger's eyes widened and her face got red. "What?"

"You didn't pay your deposit," Lauren explained gently. "It looks like you didn't have money with you, but Fisk took you at your word and purchased materials for the project. You still haven't come up with the money, so your project can't be completed ahead of others who have paid."

Hands on hips, Mrs. Wittinger glared from him to Lauren and back again. "I'm giving business to you. You should be grateful."

"I am—" Fisk started to say.

"Fisk is extremely busy," Lauren interrupted him, giving Mrs. Wittinger a stern, teacher-like frown. "We have to prioritize projects that have paid down payments."

"Are you the so-called office manager?"

"Nothing so-called about it," Lauren said easily. She shifted the baby to the other side and held out a hand. "Lauren Kantz. And I actually unearthed an old credit card machine, if you'd like to pay today. That would get you back on the list."

Mrs. Wittinger's mouth opened and closed.

Fisk felt like the expression on his own face was the same. He started to say, "Oh, it's—" but Lauren gave him a small hand-wave, indicating he should be quiet.

He obeyed.

"Oh, fine," Mrs. Wittinger said. "How much is it?"

"Come on over to the desk, and I'll get you the exact figure. We can take care of the deposit, and I'll put you back on the list."

As they talked, Lauren charmed the older woman back into being cheerful, and Fisk smiled and got back to work.

It felt nice to have someone defend him.

Too nice.

He needed to remember that no matter how good his working relationship with Lauren became, he'd never deserve anything more. Anything personal. Anything permanent.

He rubbed Nemo's side and the dog leaned against him, and he refocused on working hard to build furniture and rebuild his reputation in Holiday Point.

Chapter Four

"You're matchmaking, aren't you?" Lauren faced down her grandfather on Friday night, hands on hips.

"Now, what would give you that idea?" Gramps's eyes twinkled as he puttered around his kitchen, slowly cleaning up after dinner.

"Let me help you with that." She took the sponge out of his hand and started wiping down the kitchen table, shaking her head, fighting a smile. "It's a good thing you're so handsome," she said. "Otherwise, I'd be madder than I am about you making excuses not to go."

He'd claimed to be lonely and desperate to go to a holiday light show that he used to attend every year with Gram. Lauren had agreed, and then Gramps had gotten Fisk to drive, saying the view was better from a high-up truck than from a sedan-type car like he and Lauren both had.

Now he was backing out entirely, leaving Lauren to go with Fisk. Just Fisk. The two of them.

There was a rap on the back door.

Gramps opened it and welcomed Fisk in. Lauren sucked in a breath at the sight of the man in well-fitting jeans, a leather jacket and boots. Fisk looked good every day, even in his old work clothes. But now, clean-shaven and a little more dressed up, he looked…amazing.

"Listen, I'm going to stay here with Bonita," Gramps said to Fisk. "She's gone to sleep and she needs it. She's still a little under the weather. You two go ahead."

Fisk looked at Lauren. "What do you think?"

"I think it's strange that Gramps suddenly changed his mind," she said.

"She thinks I'm matchmaking," Gramps said.

Something crossed Fisk's face.

"But I would never do that," Gramps fibbed, oblivious. "I just think the two of you have been working hard. A lot harder than me. You should go, and I'll catch the show when the senior group goes next week."

"The senior group is going next week? You acted like this was the only chance you'd ever have to see the light show." Lauren shook her head. "Why do I listen to anything you say?"

Gramps took her coat off the hook by the door and held it for her. "Go. Have fun. I do have an ulterior motive. I want you to figure out how great Holiday Point is so that you decide to stay long-term." There was something heartfelt in his words, despite their joking tone.

What could she say to that? She stuck her arms into her coat sleeves and the decision was made.

As they drove, Lauren realized that something about Fisk was different, missing. "Where's Nemo?"

"I left him home tonight."

"You can do that?" So far, Nemo had been close to Fisk's side every time she'd seen him.

Fisk nodded. "I managed for a good while without a dog," he said. "Well, *managed* might not be the right word. I had some flashbacks and things of that sort, related to my time in the service. Self-medicated with alcohol."

"Ah. That makes sense." The alcohol couldn't have done him any good, but she could understand why he'd felt the need.

"It was only when I dried out and got some counseling that I realized a dog might help. I got Nemo just a couple of months ago. I don't want to make him work all the time, nor rely on him whenever I leave the house."

"Makes sense." She already liked the perky, intelligent dog, but she could see Fisk's point.

When they reached the fairgrounds and drove through the pay booth, illuminations stretched as far as Lauren could see. Colorful animals and blocks were outlined in lights. At the center, a glowing blue Christmas tree dominated the rest of the show. Blinking visions of Santa and his reindeer lined the side of the road. There were snowmen that moved, decorating a tree while snowflakes flashed around them.

Back in Harrisburg, Lauren had moved in elite circles where elegant holiday parties were more the norm. A simple pleasure like an outdoor light show had not been on her social agenda.

She realized she had a lot to learn about small-town life and a lot of it was good. She saw people she already recognized, working the displays.

Fisk's eyes were lit up with wonder, too, as he steered them slowly through.

"There's a place we can park," he said. "Do you want to stay a little while or are you in a hurry to get back?"

The thought of being in a parked car with Fisk, in a Hallmark-like holiday environment, raised her heart rate.

He was watching her with an unreadable expression on his face. Could he tell what she was thinking? "See, over there," he said, gesturing. "There's a fire, and you can make your own s'mores. There are some singers, I think. But it's up to you."

Of course, he didn't mean anything romantic by it. That was her own silly imagination, sparked by the beautiful surroundings and the warm mood of a holiday. "Sure," she said, hoping she sounded neutral. "Let's do it."

They grabbed the supplies for s'mores and then sat on a bench by the fire. There were other family groups and couples, but the lights here were dim and Fisk and Lauren were mostly hidden in the flickering firelight. The smell of the woodsmoke, the sound of the carolers singing "Mary, Did You Know?" the flickering lights and gentle conversations in the background, all of it transported her away from her cares. But, dangerously, the environment brought her closer to Fisk.

They leaned forward and roasted their marshmallows. When hers caught on fire and dropped down into the coals, he laughed and handed her another one, to which she did the same thing.

"Here," he said. He pulled his own perfectly browned marshmallow off the stick and held it out to her. Rather than putting it onto her waiting s'more, she popped it into her mouth. Yum. So good. Her eyes closed as she tasted the gooey sweetness.

When she opened her eyes, he was looking at her, his expression speculative.

Her face heated. She looked away and leaned back, only to realize that his arm was along the back of the bench.

Her mind told her to move away, jerk away, get away. Except…it felt good. She stole a glance at him.

He was watching her, a tentative smile on his face.

A man approached them. "Hey, Wilkins. You gonna break things up again this year?"

The light went out of Fisk's expression. He withdrew his arm and stood. "No, sir," he said to the older man who'd spoken. "But if there's any way I can make up for what I did last year, I'd like to do that."

The man looked thoughtful. "Sobered up, have you?"

Fisk nodded. "With the help of God and AA."

"Then, we could use a hand repairing some of the figures that got damaged in that ice storm we had."

"I'll start tomorrow. Just tell me where to show up."

They walked over toward a shed, and Lauren propped her chin on her fists, watching them.

She wanted to grab Fisk and tell him he needed to work on his own business, not take on unrelated, volunteer commitments. She also wanted to tell him that he was a good guy, whatever had happened, whatever his reputation.

But that might just be her codependence talking. Who knew what Fisk might have done in this town before he got sober? Maybe he wasn't a good guy. She couldn't be sure, not yet anyway.

She needed to remember that any attraction she felt to Fisk probably came from an unhealthy place. She needed to pay attention to the fact that his alcoholic escapades were still fresh in people's minds.

She needed to keep her distance, no matter how difficult that was to do.

Fisk was in the shop working at 7 a.m. on Saturday, Nemo conked out at his side. The quiet, the dawn appearing through the windows, the crisp, cool air, all of it put him into a contemplative frame of mind. He wasn't much for sitting still and praying. Instead, on a morning like this, he communed with God while his hands were busy setting out the day's supplies and pulling his first project to the center of his work area.

At 8:15, he heard a screech of tires. Nemo jerked upright, barked and rushed to the window. There was a pounding on his door, and then the laughing presence of his brothers as they entered the workshop.

"Put your tools away, we're going fishing!" Cam said.

Fisk didn't get up from his workbench. "I'm not. Can't."

"Our wives want to shop today and our kids are going to this all-day church program. Weather is good."

"It's December!" Fisk protested. "45 degrees and cloudy. Rain coming later."

"Perfect for trout fishing," Alec said. "Come on."

Nemo ran in circles around them, yipping. Without his service vest, he was acting like a puppy.

"I can't," Fisk said over Nemo's noise. He gestured around the shop, where projects in various states of completion nearly filled the space. He did regret it, though. He treasured his improved relationship with his brothers. Funny how, when you sobered up and started treating people right, relationships got better.

His brothers had been nothing but supportive when he'd gone through his worst times, but now they related more as equals.

"What did I miss?" Lauren came through the side door, wearing faded jeans and a fleece jacket, Bonita on her hip. A couple of file folders looked about to overflow the leather satchel she was carrying.

His brothers immediately went nuts over Bonita. You wouldn't have thought it from how rough they'd grown up, but it turned out they all loved babies.

Fisk remembered the weight of Scarlett in his arms.

He wandered over to the wide awning windows and

looked out into the misty, early-morning light. He cranked a window open and breathed in crisp, pine-scented air. It would be nice to get outside.

"Fisk can take a day off, right?" Cam was asking Lauren.

Nemo yipped, sitting bolt upright in front of Fisk, watching his every move.

Fisk turned before Lauren could speak. He didn't want her to have to be the heavy. "I have too much to do," he told Cam and Alec. "Christmas orders."

"You should go." Lauren set the baby down on a rug beside her desk and handed her a couple of plastic toys. "You need to have fun. It'll make you more creative."

"I can't go off fishing while you're here working," he protested, walking over to the office area.

"You should go shopping with our wives," Alec said, pulling out his phone.

"No, thanks. Go on." She waved a hand, shooing all of them away. "I'm only working a couple of hours. I'll get a little done, and then Gramps and I are going to visit some relatives I haven't seen in ages."

Her hair, down around her shoulders, looked blonder than usual in the morning light. She wasn't wearing makeup. When the baby cried out, she leaned over and swept her into her arms easily, then perched her on her knee. "Wave bye-bye," she told Bonita.

She was ordering him out of his own shop, and he loved it. He wouldn't mind having a woman like Lauren boss him around all the time.

His brothers teased him most of the way to Caseman's Creek.

"You're so under her thumb," Alec said.

"She sounds like a wife." Cam steered off the main road and they started jolting down a dirt one.

A wife. Longing rose in his heart, but he squelched it. "Can it. She's not my wife and she's not going to be."

His brothers glanced at each other.

Then Alec smacked Cam's arm. "You're driving like Old Granny Wilkins," he said.

Challenge accepted. "Didn't want to scare you," Cam said as he stepped on the gas. Alec whooped, and they bumped and bounced over the unpaved road.

Sitting beside Nemo in the back seat, Fisk let out a whoop of his own, suddenly transported back to his teenage years. They'd spent many days skipping school, riding out to Meadow Run, catching food for dinner, ignoring the laws. They'd been poachers. They hadn't known any better.

It had been some fun times, but now was different. Now they were men and understood the reasons for hunting and fishing laws. As soon as they parked, Alec started lecturing them on changes in the fishing regulations. They all pinned their licenses on their caps and headed toward their old favorite spots.

Fisk's breath made clouds in the air as he pushed through laurel branches to a flat rock that overlooked the river. Nemo explored alongside him, sniffing everything, getting sticks and burrs in his coat. Overhead, bare tree branches traced a lacy pattern against the sky.

God's in His heaven, all's right with the world. His mom had used to say it on pretty fall mornings, walking them to the bus stop in her Cupid's Cleaners uniform. Fisk couldn't have been more than five.

He wondered if Lauren would stay in the area long enough to walk Bonita to the school bus stop.

"Only thing missing is Frank," Alec said. He'd put on

waders and walked a little ways out into the stream, just like always. Trying to get to the best spot.

Fisk glanced over at the section of bank where their other brother liked to fish. "Frank needs to get back up here for a visit," he said. "Mom and Dad aren't getting any younger."

"Any smarter, either," Alec muttered.

"Mom would come around if Dad didn't pull her back down all the time." Cam cast upriver.

"She'll never leave him." That was Alec.

"She loves him," Fisk said.

"Yeah, but...love can be bad for you." Alec's words made them all go quiet. Fisk thought about his own mistakes in love.

Cam flipped water at Fisk, then at Alec. "Lighten up and catch some fish."

Fisk ended up pulling in a big, gorgeous trout. The sun flashed out from behind the clouds just as he netted it, illuminating its pink-and-black scales.

His mouth watered at the thought of a fresh trout dinner.

It was so beautiful, though. So alive.

The way it moved, the curve of its tail... Fisk's fingers itched to capture the creature in wood.

He held the fish and carefully extracted the hook, then, regretfully, tossed it back into the stream.

"Why'd you do that?" Cam demanded. "That would've been good eating."

"Why even fish if you're going to release a beauty like that?" Alec sounded disgusted.

"You're not wrong." Fisk regretted the fresh trout dinner he'd given up. But he'd had to do it.

There was what he wanted, and there was the right thing to do. They didn't always match up.

He couldn't really explain it to his irate brothers, nor to

himself. He just knew he had plenty and didn't need the fish for food. In that situation, it felt right to let one of God's beautiful creatures go on living.

He looked off downstream, shading his eyes. A fish jumped once, twice. Fisk thought—hoped, anyway—it was the one he'd set free.

Chapter Five

Sunday afternoon was blustery, with snow blowing sideways and whistling through the pines around the Holiday Point church. Lauren would have expected everyone in town to hurry home after services. But that hadn't happened. After an all-church meal, most members of the congregation had stayed, packing the fellowship hall. Now, enthusiastic people made Christmas crafts at various stations around the large room.

Apparently, the Christmas crafts workshop had been a tradition for years. On a Sunday in December, everyone gathered at the church to make decorations or gifts for the holidays. At each table, one or two people were skilled craftspeople who knew what they were doing. Everyone else learned as they went, with some comical results.

Lauren strolled through, intrigued. Since her family had only visited Gramps during the summers, she'd never experienced a Holiday Point Christmas. And she loved it. Every day seemed to bring more opportunities to gather with neighbors and do something fun and positive.

This craft workshop was a case in point. It seemed to have drawn everyone in town.

Most of the women were making intricate ornaments or mantel decor, but Lauren was drawn to a bird feeder station.

She'd like to make a couple of bird feeders, one for herself and Bonita, who was safely napping in the church nursery, and one for Gramps, for him to hang outside the window by his favorite chair. She'd never worked with wood, but these days with Fisk had given her an interest, and she liked the smell of the wood, the feel of it. She picked up one of the precut pieces and turned it over in her hands.

A telltale yip alerted her to the presence of Nemo, and thus of Fisk. She turned to find both of them beside her.

"Thinking of making a birdhouse?" he asked in his husky voice. "I can help."

The offer set her heart beating faster. Which was ridiculous. She worked with Fisk every day, so what was different about learning to make a birdhouse from him?

"You should do something different," she told him. "You work with wood all week."

"I *should* be home working on my orders," he said. "Normally, I take Sundays off, but since I played hooky yesterday, fishing with my brothers, I need to catch up."

"You do," she said.

"But—" he shrugged "—when the church asked, how could I say no?"

"Are *you* the person helping with the carpentry station?" The voice behind them was sultry, breathy, suggestive. "Could you teach me?"

Lauren turned to see a pretty blonde dressed in a too-tight-for-church dress. Could she even sit down in that thing, let alone do a craft?

The woman wasn't looking at Lauren, though. She only had eyes for Fisk.

"Hey, Tonya," he said, sounding relaxed and friendly. "Have you met Lauren Kantz? She's new in town."

"Nice to meet you," Lauren said.

Tonya's eyes flickered from Fisk to Lauren and back again. "Likewise," she said, her voice still breathy, and took a step closer to Fisk.

Nemo barked and nudged his way between Fisk and Tonya.

Lauren loved that dog.

"Have a seat," Fisk said easily. "You too, Lauren. I'll teach you both to make a birdhouse. It's pretty simple, since the pieces are all precut."

Tonya shimmied into one of the chairs, adjusting her dress. Lauren sat down beside her. She was glad she'd worn casual pants and a sweater, mostly—it was a comfortable outfit for this type of activity—but a part of her wished she'd taken a little more time with her appearance. Tonya was made up to the hilt, her hair beautifully curled, and she made it obvious that she was interested in Fisk.

Lauren didn't want to think about why she didn't like that.

Fisk sat on the other side of the table, Nemo beside him. "Okay. Each of you needs a base, sides and a roof." He nodded toward the stacks of precut wood on the table. "Choose the wood that speaks to you."

Suspicion rose in Lauren. "This is what you were doing when you went back to the shop last night." She'd seen the light on there when she'd gone to bed after eleven.

"Guilty," he said, laughing. "I waited until the last minute and had to catch up. Didn't want to disappoint my church friends."

Tonya looked from one to the other. "Are you two living together?"

"No," Lauren said.

"Nope." Fisk was pulling out supplies from a box beneath the table. "We're neighbors, and Lauren is helping me get my business organized. Doing a great job of it, too," he added, smiling at her.

Lauren's insides swirled. That smile was lethal.

"Oh, that's right, I heard about you," Tonya said, picking up a piece of wood and looking at it. "You're running away from some scandal, right?"

Lauren sucked in a breath and looked quickly at Fisk. He raised an eyebrow but didn't comment.

Did that mean he knew? Or was curious? Or didn't care? "I... I'd rather not talk about it," she said to Tonya. "In fact, I'd appreciate if you didn't say anything about it to anyone else in town."

"Sure," Tonya said easily. She picked up another piece of wood. "Believe me, I know about scandal. It's my middle name in this town."

Fisk smiled at her. "You and me, both."

The two of them seemed to share a bond, and it made Lauren curious. "Have you two been friends a long time?"

Tonya laughed. "Didn't we meet in the principal's office in like second grade?"

"Probably. I spent enough time there." Fisk was stacking wooden pegs in front of both of them. "The Wilkinses were more notorious than the Mitfords, but not by much."

"It was just that there were more of you," Tonya said. "I'm an only child," she explained to Lauren. "My dad kind of went through the women."

"And our dads were drinking buddies." Fisk pulled out a diagram and set it where they could see it. "You start with attaching the two sides to the front with wood glue. Like so." He stood his own demonstration pieces together.

Lauren and Tonya did as he'd done, only more clumsily.

"Pretty sure our dads robbed a convenience store together once," Tonya said.

Lauren's eyes widened and she looked at Fisk for confirmation.

A flush darkened his cheeks, but he nodded. "You may be right. My brothers would know. But who wants to dredge all that up?"

"Not me," Tonya said. "My dad's in the big house now. I don't need to analyze how he got started."

"I didn't know he'd gotten convicted." Fisk showed them how to gently pound pegs through the precut holes in the face of the birdhouse and into the edge of each wall.

For several minutes, they focused on their work while Christmas music and friendly, excited voices swirled around them.

"Flip the assembly now, and we'll glue on the back and do the same thing there." Fisk demonstrated.

"How's your dad doing, anyway?" Tonya asked as she held her pieces crookedly together.

Fisk glanced at Lauren. "Not sure if you really want to hear about our family's, uh, shadier activities."

That flush across his cheekbones was still there. *He's embarrassed*, she realized. But she admired the way he wasn't backing away from the truth or denying it.

She could learn something from him, and Tonya, too, she realized. Except that robbing a convenience store was nothing compared to what her husband had done.

Which Tonya must know about, since she'd brought up the scandal. "I have no room to judge anyone's family," she said. "And you probably can't shock me."

"Really." Fisk lifted an eyebrow.

"Really. So you can tell us about your dad."

Tonya shot her a smile as if to say she realized how Lauren had dodged talking about her own past. "Yeah," she said. "Tell us about your dad, Fisk. I always thought he was a nice guy, sober."

"We're all a lot nicer sober," Fisk said. "It just took a while for me to realize that. My dad's not there yet, but I haven't heard of him doing anything criminal for at least a couple of years."

"Progress, not perfection," Tonya said with a snort. "Speaking of, what's wrong with my birdhouse? It looks kind of…tilted."

"Mine, too." Lauren studied her own birdhouse. Maybe this would be the one she made for practice, and she could do another, better one for Gramps.

Around them, talk and laughter rose as people created their crafts at the various stations. A couple of kids ran by, then skidded to a halt beside Nemo. "Can we pet him?" the little girl asked.

"Good to ask before touching a working dog." Fisk slipped off Nemo's vest. "I think Nemo's ready for a break."

"You mean he was working? He looked like he was taking a nap!"

"That's the kind of job you wanna get, kids," Tonya said. "One where you can take naps on the clock."

Lauren couldn't help laughing. Tonya was different, but Lauren liked her.

She just wondered about Fisk's attitude toward Tonya. After being around them, she got more of a friend vibe than a romantic one, despite Tonya's attire and sultry approach.

Even if the two of them did have feelings for one another, it wasn't Lauren's business. She couldn't let herself develop a romantic interest in a man like Fisk, who had a drinking problem. She knew from her therapist that was too dangerous a route for her to go.

But as the three of them finished the birdhouses together

and laughed at Lauren and Tonya's obviously amateur projects, Lauren felt bemused. She was starting to make some friends here in Holiday Point and to feel like a part of it. Someone like Tonya, whose past wasn't pristine, and yet who didn't hold Lauren's own past against her, made her feel comfortable.

She wanted to belong. Wanted it so much she ached; wanted it for herself and for Bonita.

Maybe this could work, so long as she didn't get too terribly caught up in the fluttery feelings she was having for Fisk.

On Monday morning, Fisk got to the shop early, primed to get a lot done. It was already December 9, which meant he had just over two weeks to get everything completed for Christmas. Thanks to the schedule Lauren had made for him, he knew he could do it…but only if nothing went wrong and he didn't take any more breaks to fish with his brothers or help out at church.

As he readied a corner cabinet for final sanding, he reflected on yesterday's Christmas crafts workshop. No, he hadn't really had time to do it, but he liked sharing his skills with others.

Especially others like Lauren, his inner, most honest voice reminded him.

Nemo sidled up, and he ran a hand over the dog's shaggy fur. He'd seen a different side of Lauren yesterday. Most women shunned Tonya due to her tight clothes and flirtatious ways, which was one reason Fisk sometimes felt sorry for Tonya and tried to include her.

Lauren had been nice to her. Not in a charitable way, either, but as if the two of them could become actual friends.

Fisk liked that about Lauren. She wasn't judgmental and she wasn't a snob.

Of course she isn't. Otherwise, she wouldn't be working for you.

He was halfway done with sanding the cabinet when Lauren burst through the door, letting in cold, sunny air. Bonita was tucked under one arm like a sack of potatoes, but true to her cheerful personality, she was laughing, evidently enjoying her sideways view of the world.

Fisk went over and closed the door behind them, then swung Bonita down and set her on her feet. She promptly sat and tried to pull off her gloves and hat.

Fisk helped Lauren off with her coat and resisted the temptation to touch her windblown hair. He hung her coat on a hook by the door. "I see we have a new coworker today," he said, kneeling beside Bonita and tickling her under the chin.

"I'm sorry about that," Lauren said. "Gramps isn't feeling well and I figured he could use a break. If she gets too active, I can take her home."

"We agreed that you could bring her to work as necessary." He watched the baby, as she looked around, wide-eyed, then crawled toward Nemo, who was stretching beside Fisk.

His arms ached to hold Bonita, but he didn't pick her up again. Instead, he updated Lauren on what he'd been working on and his plans for the day. Then he forced himself to turn away and get back to work. He tried to ignore the pleasant, singsong sound of Lauren's voice as she talked to Bonita, pointing out animals in a board book.

He finished sanding the cabinet and put on the first coat of stain, the pungent smell and the beauty of the wood grain keeping him in the moment. As he moved on to his next project, though, Bonita's cries penetrated his consciousness. He looked over.

Lauren was trying to hold her cell phone against her ear while bouncing Bonita on her knee, and Bonita wasn't having it.

Drawn as if by a magnet, he went over and took Bonita out of Lauren's arms.

Thank you, she mouthed, and handed him an open diaper bag full of Bonita's things.

It was a tiny, domestic moment. Awareness flashed between them.

Fisk realized that just as he'd had domestic times with his girlfriend and baby, Lauren must have had the same with her ex. He felt the sudden urge to listen in on her personal phone call, to find out if that was who she was speaking to. What was her relationship to Bonita's dad? How ex, exactly, was he?

He walked Bonita over toward the windows, closing his ears to the sound of Lauren's voice. Swaying with the baby, he pointed out a bright red cardinal flitting from branch to branch, and Bonita chortled with laughter, her fussing forgotten.

He settled the baby on his knee and tried to focus on polishing a section of a bench, one-handed. That worked for a little while. But Bonita was an active baby, and Fisk was all too willing to put his work aside and entertain her with toys from her well-organized diaper bag: a pretend cell phone and a small stuffed bear.

When she got tired of those, he rummaged in the diaper bag for food. He found a container of yellow puffs, tried one, and made a face at Bonita. "Tasteless," he said.

"Puh! Puh!" She reached for the container.

He pulled her up into his lap and spread a few puffs on his hand. She grabbed one and threw it on the floor.

Nemo raced over and scarfed it down.

Bonita grabbed another puff and did the same thing. And again. And again.

Lauren was still on the phone, but she was watching them. When Fisk looked her way, she gave him a smile and a thumbs-up.

The sweetness of the moment got to Fisk. His heart ached, but in a half-pleasant way.

After a little while, Bonita got fussy again, and he riffled through the diaper bag to see if Lauren had packed any better snacks. She had. Several, actually: cubes of cheese, whole grain crackers, a container of applesauce and a little spoon. Bonita reached for the applesauce, saying "Ah-sas!"

He spooned it into her mouth, then let her try holding the spoon herself. That got applesauce into her hair as well as her mouth, and they both laughed as he tried to wipe her down.

An impossible mix of feelings washed through him. Happiness, because she was so adorable that you couldn't help but smile to see her. Regret, because he and Di hadn't ever had this kind of carefully organized diaper bag or multiple healthy snacks.

Grief, because Scarlett wasn't here and would never grow beyond this stage, would never learn to run or talk, would never go to school or camp or prom, would never get a job or become a mother.

He wiped Bonita's face and then used a corner of the cloth to wipe his own eyes.

Someone pounded on the door. Lauren was still on the phone, so he hiked Bonita onto his hip and went to answer it.

Uh-oh. Mrs. Wittinger.

"I see you're still playing house rather than working," she scolded, stepping inside. Her boots dripped slushy snow onto the mat and beyond.

Fisk blew out a breath. "What can I do for you?"

"I'd like to make a change to my order." She proceeded to list three or four features she wanted different in the cabinet she'd ordered: paint color, scallops rather than straight edges, an additional shelf.

He reached for his phone and made a voice note, groaning internally. All of that would take time he didn't have.

"I certainly hope the project will be ready on schedule, even though you appear to be spending most of your time with your baby," she said.

Your baby. The words almost derailed him. He took a deep breath.

God, grant me the serenity to accept the things I cannot change.

He couldn't change what had happened to Di and Scarlett. And he couldn't change Mrs. Wittinger. She'd be impatient and demanding until the day she went to meet her maker, unless that same maker caused her a change of heart.

With that awareness came the serenity he'd prayed for. "I can make those adjustments," he said, "but they'll delay your order until after the holidays."

"What?" She put a hand on her hip.

Bonita reached for her, laughing. "Wat, wat," she echoed.

Fisk managed to restrain a laugh, but not a smile. "We can keep the order as is and it'll be delivered on time, or we can make these changes and I'll finish it after the holidays. Your call."

"Fine. Leave it as is." She turned and stalked out the door, slamming it behind her.

"Well done!" Lauren came up behind him. "I'm so proud of you for standing up to her."

He grinned. "I only did it because you weren't available to beard the lion yourself," he said.

"Ma! Ma!" Bonita said.

Lauren held out her hands and he handed the baby over.

Fisk's arms felt empty without her. He supposed they'd always feel empty.

"Thank you for taking care of her. I never expected that call to go on so long." They turned together and walked back into the office portion of the shop, Fisk grabbing the diaper bag along the way.

Lauren sat down behind the desk, Bonita in her arms. She cuddled her and leaned back and tickled her toes, making them both laugh.

Such a bond they had. Lauren was a great mom.

Di had never focused this intently on Scarlett. She'd loved her baby, but she'd been more into partying.

And Fisk needed to stop comparing the two women. He'd aided and abetted Di's partying. Neither he nor Di had grown up in the kind of homes that put kids first. Di hadn't known any better, and neither had Fisk. But he was glad that Lauren was a different kind of parent and was raising her baby so well.

He knew he should get back to work, but he was having a hard time making himself do it. "I hope everything's okay," he said. "Your phone call sounded stressful."

"It was," she said, her expression going wary. "I, well, it had to do with my divorce settlement."

"Your ex?" he asked.

She shook her head. "He doesn't get to make too many phone calls, and I wouldn't take them if he did," she said.

"He's in prison, and I hope he stays there for a long, long time."

Fisk stared as his impression of Lauren underwent another transformation. What had her husband done that had put him in prison?

Chapter Six

Lauren watched Fisk, her nerves tightening.

This was the moment she hated: when people found out that her ex was in prison. It was topped only when they discovered what he was in prison for.

Why had she announced Jeff's prison status to Fisk?

She fussed with Bonita's shoes and then put her down to practice walking on the floor, holding her little hands. When people learned what her ex had done, they were rightly horrified. That horror tended to spill over onto Lauren and Bonita.

Lauren needed to keep Bonita safe, and that meant keeping her father's crimes a secret. "I shouldn't have even mentioned that," she said to Fisk. "He's out of my life. It's just, the lawyers are dickering over some terms of the settlement, and I want to get all the help for Bonita that I can."

Fisk nodded. He wasn't acting appalled that her husband was in prison, which was a nice change from some people. "Will Bonita be able to visit him?"

"No. No way." That had been an easy enough term to get into the divorce agreement. "I have full custody, and for her to see her father at this point would be detrimental. Once she's of age, and can understand what happened, she can choose to see him if she wants. But until then, no way."

"He must have done something pretty bad." Fisk's voice was mild, his eyes curious. "Hurt you badly, too."

The gentle words unlocked something in Lauren. They made her remember a time when she'd loved Jeff, when she'd watched him performing on stage and felt like the queen of the world because she was his wife. He'd been so very handsome, so charming.

And Fisk was right: as his true colors had come to the surface, it had hurt her. Scarred her, even. "You're not wrong," she said. "I dreamed of having a different life, a good life, with him and Bonita. Losing that does hurt." Her throat tightened up and she looked away.

He reached out and gave her forearm a brief squeeze. It was just an effort to comfort her, she knew that, but nonetheless, it warmed her.

Warmed her a little too much, but still, she didn't pull back.

When she looked at his face, he was watching her, and there was...something. Something in his eyes.

Oh, wow. This could go way, way off track. She scooted her chair away, making a loud screech and startling Bonita, whose face screwed up to cry.

Immediately, Fisk leaned forward. "B-b-b-bonita," he said, half singing the words. He picked up one of the toys she'd flung down and rattled it.

Bonita's potential tantrum turned into a smile.

"Ba-ba-ba-ba-ba!" she sang out.

And that provided the perfect change of topic. "How'd you get to be so good with babies?" Lauren asked him.

He shrugged, his smile fading. He handed the toy to Bonita. "I'd better get back to work," he said, and walked over to his latest project. Nemo, who'd seemed to be sound asleep a minute ago, got to his feet and trotted after Fisk.

Maybe her question about his experience with babies had been too personal. She didn't know much about his past. Maybe he was one of the many men who'd lost touch with his children in a divorce.

She walked over and perched beside the spot where he was working. "I'm sorry if that question was intrusive. I get having a past you don't want to talk about."

He glanced at her, glanced away, and then looked back. "Let's stay in the present for now," he said.

She held up an imaginary glass as if for a toast. "To the present," she said.

Their eyes met and held.

Lauren's heart started pounding, double-time. His eyes were gray-blue, and so intense that she had to look away.

She sucked in a breath. "We need to stay in the present for your work," she said, hearing the breathy sound of her own voice. "There's a lot to do."

"Uh-huh," he said huskily, and cleared his throat. "Lots of reasons the present is a good place to be."

His gaze locked on her face. She could see the rise and fall of his chest.

Everything inside her reached out to him with a longing she didn't even understand. He was a handsome man, maybe even a good man, but there was more to this. He was more compelling than anyone she'd ever met before.

And then… Ohhhh. Of course. How many light bulb moments did she have to have before it sank in?

He was compelling because she had a problem. Her own codependency problem. "Um, I'd better go check on Gramps."

"Sure." His expression went bland. "That's fine. If you want to work from there this afternoon, keep an eye on him and Bonita, that's fine."

"I think I'll…do that." She still felt breathless as she escaped out the door.

* * *

She thought about it all afternoon. Couldn't help it, really; the image of his face, his gaze, kept intruding into her mind.

He was *so* intense. So complicated. So full of untapped depth.

So dangerous.

Too dangerous. She shouldn't stay. She should run as fast as she could away from him, lest she get involved in another terrible situation, dealing with the mess from a troubled man's issues.

And yet, apart from Fisk himself, this situation was ideal. Now, for example. She was working on her laptop at the kitchen table while Gramps dozed on the couch, a TV show playing quietly. Bonita was in the bedroom, having her nap.

What other job would afford her the opportunity to do so much for Bonita and Gramps and still earn a living wage?

But if she let herself be caught up in Fisk's magnetism, it would undo the work she'd done in therapy. If she went down that rabbit hole again, she couldn't be a good mother to Bonita.

Her feelings were exciting now, and starting up a relationship with him would be exciting too, at first. Even now, she felt a shivery thrill at the idea. The way he'd looked at her... She'd read it clearly enough. He was definitely interested.

But getting involved with an alcoholic was a slippery slope she'd been down before. She'd lose her boundaries and make herself responsible for Fisk's feelings. She'd try to fix him without success. She'd put aside her own interests, and she'd be loyal way beyond the point that she should.

So did she quit her job and move far, far away?

She'd done that before. She'd run away from her ex.

And she'd landed in the path of another handsome, compelling alcoholic.

Apparently, there were a lot of them around. She should have known it from her childhood. Her father had been charming and fun, always surrounded by a lot of other fun people. When the spotlight of his attention had fallen on her, his only daughter, it had been the best thing ever.

He'd charmed her mother. He'd charmed plenty of other women, too, as he'd drunk himself into cirrhosis of the liver and an early grave.

And Lauren had gone directly into the arms of another charming alcoholic.

She propped her cheek on her fist and looked out the window. Bare trees made a lacy pattern against the sky's cloudy grayness. A blue jay hopped from branch to branch of a pine tree, cawing.

For now, at least through the holiday season, she'd stay. But she'd keep her eyes open for other opportunities. After the first of the year, she'd reassess.

It would be ideal to live in the region. Gramps was happier having her nearby, and she wanted to be here for him. Holiday Point was a good town, would be a good place for Bonita to grow up.

She lowered her head and prayed for the strength to make and carry out the right decision, and to avoid getting caught up in the unhealthy patterns of the past.

Fisk sensed it: something was different with Lauren. She was here, and yet she wasn't. Ever since that day when Fisk had come so close to kissing her.

They were driving down snowy backroads in his truck, on the way home from delivering several of his Christmas projects. Fisk felt good about that; all three customers had raved about his handiwork. Plus, he now had money in his pocket. Not really in his pocket, he reminded himself. It would mostly go back into the business. But it was good to be earning, to watch money come in as well as go out.

He hesitated, debating with himself. But the turnoff was coming. Decision time. "Do you mind making one more stop?"

From the back seat, Nemo barked.

"Nemo obviously doesn't mind," she said, laughing, "and neither do I." And then she stopped smiling and looked away from him as if the landscape suddenly held her interest.

It seemed like as soon as she caught herself having a good time, she turned off. What was that about?

But he knew what it was about: he'd come close to kissing her, had wanted to, badly. She'd sensed it and backed away.

"I'd like to deliver that wall cupboard to my parents and put it up," he said. "Preferably when they're not home, which they shouldn't be right now."

"That'll be a nice surprise."

He made the turn without telling her the real reason he hoped they weren't home. There were two of them, actually. He didn't want Lauren to meet them and maybe experience their drinking behavior. His dad, in particular, could get loud and unpleasant.

He also didn't want to be pressured to drink, himself. His recovery was going well, but it was never foolproof. He had to make good choices about what environments he spent time in.

He pulled into his parents' thankfully empty driveway. Even without them here, this environment could be triggering. He'd have plenty to talk about at his AA meeting tomorrow.

He glanced over at Lauren. Her forehead was creased. "You sure this is okay? I can drive you back if you need to get to Bonita."

"No, it's fine, it's no problem. Gramps just texted me. He has friends over and he's showing off the baby." She looked around. "Is this where you grew up?"

"Yeah." He scanned the rickety front porch, the sagging roof, the broken-down car in the yard. He thought about making a joke—something about how it wasn't exactly the Taj Mahal—but that would be covering up his true feelings, something AA counseled against. "This was home," he said instead, and got out of the car. "Do you want to stay in the car with Nemo?"

Nemo barked and pawed at the window.

"I'll come in, if you don't mind," she said. "Hanging a wall cabinet is easier with two people."

"That it is." He debated whether to bring Nemo inside, where all kinds of strange objects were probably scattered about the floor for a curious dog to sniff at and maybe consume.

The alternative was to leave Nemo out in a cold truck. A look into those dark, alert eyes decided him, and he let the dog out. "I'm trusting your training," he said to the dog. "Stay by me and don't touch anything."

Nemo barked in response, and Lauren laughed. "I think Nemo understands English," she said.

"I think so, too." He rubbed his dog's head, grateful for the comfort provided.

Lauren helped him carry the cabinet inside and didn't comment on the ripped cushion in the recliner or the heap of dirty dishes in the kitchen. When he unwrapped the cabinet, though, she gasped audibly. "It's beautiful!" she said. "When did you make this?"

"Late nights when I couldn't sleep," he said. "I wanted to do something for my folks."

"Any particular reason you're not waiting until Christmas?" She held the cabinet in place while he eyeballed it, then made some markings on the wall.

"Christmas is a big drinking holiday for them," he said. "I didn't want it to get broken."

She winced and nodded. "I'm familiar. My dad didn't break things, not physically at least, but holidays weren't a happy time."

"Your dad drank? Did he quit?"

"No. He died."

"I'm sorry."

She didn't look at him. Obviously, she didn't want to talk about it.

He got that. He didn't like talking about his childhood, either. He didn't have a lot of happy memories. His brothers had more, but things had deteriorated by the time he'd come along. Not to mention his father's attitude toward Fisk's chosen career path.

He measured the height where he wanted to place the cabinets and marked it, then located the studs, working in companionable silence with Lauren. Once, Nemo broke training and crunched down a potato chip from the floor, but a scolding word from Fisk brought him back to sit quietly beside them. Lauren was patient through all the marking and measuring, and then gamely held the cabinet while he installed the screws.

"I gotta speed this up," Fisk said as he used his drill to tighten the last screws. "They're likely to be home soon."

"You don't want to see your parents?"

He shook his head. "Even if we get along, they tend to lead me into temptation."

She made a drinking motion with her hand, raising her eyebrows, and he nodded.

He was packing up his tool bag when he heard a car pulling into the driveway. "Uh-oh," he said.

Lauren looked out the window. "Red pickup," she said, tactfully not mentioning its condition. "Looks like two people are getting out."

Great. "Like it or not," he said, "you're about to meet my parents."

Chapter Seven

Lauren stood back as Fisk's parents entered the house. His mom, wearing jeans and a Christmas sweater, crowed her excitement and threw her arms around Fisk. His father thumped him on the back, his smile genuine.

They were obviously happy to see him. But she could read Fisk's attitude: he was literally sweating as he packed up his tools.

His dad, sporting white stubble on a weathered face and long hair gathered back into a ponytail, went directly to the cabinet beside the sink. He came back with a bottle and four glasses, which he plunked down onto the kitchen table. "You gonna introduce us to your lady friend?" he asked Fisk.

Oh, Lauren definitely needed to correct that misperception. Before Fisk could answer, she walked forward and extended her hand. "Hi, Mr. Wilkins. I'm Lauren Kantz. I'm working as Fisk's office manager during the holiday season."

"Seems like I've heard that name," he said, taking her hand and shaking it. "You're a real pretty girl."

What did you say to that? She forced a smile and said nothing, hoping against hope that he wasn't a fan of the gossip rags and hadn't heard her name there, or seen a picture.

Fisk's mother came over to Lauren and took both her hands. "I'm glad to meet you," she said. "It's so good to see our Fiscus dating again."

"Uh…like I mentioned, I'm Fisk's office manager, not his date." Lauren softened the correction with a smile.

"Too bad, son." Fisk's dad clapped him on the shoulder, hard. "Now, who wants a shot?"

Fisk's mom held up her hand as if she were in school. "Me, me! It's five o'clock somewhere!" She pointed at the clock on the wall, shaped like a beer stein.

Lauren saw the time and gasped. "Is it already five? I need to get home to my daughter."

Fisk's dad guffawed and his mom laughed, too.

Fisk put a hand on her shoulder. "Don't worry," he said wryly, "it's always five o'clock here. That clock was a gift from one of Dad's drinking buddies. The time never changes. It's really only three forty-five."

She studied the clock again. "Ohhhh. Got it. Still, I need to get back soon."

"Me as well." Fisk picked up his canvas tool bag and took a couple of steps toward the door.

"Hang on," his father said. He held out a full shot glass to Fisk.

Oh, no.

Lauren saw Fisk's nostrils flare as he inhaled the strong scent of liquor. Scotch, Lauren realized; she could smell it from halfway across the room, and she had to work to conceal the way it made her stomach heave.

If it triggered that kind of reaction in her, what was it triggering in Fisk?

Her parents and her ex might have drunk a different brand than Fisk's parents, but it was basically the same stuff and had the same effect. Not a good one.

She should let Fisk make his own decision, but he seemed to be having trouble doing so. His hand lifted toward the glass.

She walked over and took Fisk's arm. "Come on, I need to leave now. I have to get home to Bonita." She smiled apologetically at Fisk's parents while tugging at his arm.

He blinked. "She's right, we do need to go."

"One shot doesn't take but a sec." Fisk's father illustrated the truth of his statement by lifting a shot glass to his own lips and tossing it down.

"I'm not drinking, Dad, remember?" Fisk's voice was steady, but Lauren could hear the slightest tremor in it.

How had she gotten to know him so well, in just a couple of weeks, that she could read his unspoken emotions?

"Aw, you're no fun anymore." Fisk's father made a disgusted face. "Figures. You always were a wuss."

Fisk, a *wuss*? She looked at his impassive face and read the pain underneath. Again…how had she gotten to where she could understand him so well?

Nemo broke the tension with a few sharp yips.

"Yeah, you need to get home, too, don't you?" Lauren said to him. "It was nice to meet you both. Come on, Fisk." She pulled at his arm.

He followed her outside, where a cold wind had started up. Nemo trotted close beside him, clearly sensing that Fisk needed comfort.

Fisk helped her into the truck and then walked around and let Nemo in. He got into the driver's seat and put the truck into gear, then turned toward her. "So that's my folks," he said flatly. "Thanks for getting me out of there."

She thought of something and sucked in a breath. "They didn't even notice the cabinet."

Fisk shrugged. "They will." As he backed out of the

driveway and started down the road, he glanced over at her. "You saved me in there. I wanted that drink, badly. Still do."

Lauren scrunched a little away from him, close to the door. She'd gotten her husband out of numerous tempting situations, and she'd grown up watching her mother do the same for her dad.

Now, while the escape was being made, was an important moment, she knew that. All too often, it would go bad. The alcoholic would resent whomever had gotten them out of the situation and would use that emotion as an excuse to stop at a bar.

That was why it was better to let the recovering person make their own decision about whether or not to take a drink. Making a decision strengthened you, while being told what to do weakened you. "I'm sorry I kind of took over in there," she said. "I just didn't want to see you take the one drink."

"I can't," Fisk said. "One will lead to more and more."

"I understand." And she did, all too well.

Fisk was an alcoholic, just like her father and her husband. His moment of wavering in his parents' house just proved it.

And yes, she knew how to deal with a person with a drinking problem. She'd had plenty of experience doing it, way too much. It was a role she felt comfortable in. She was actually proud she'd gotten him out of there.

She'd controlled the situation. That was what codependents did with their addicted partners.

And it was a role she absolutely needed to stay away from. "If it's okay with you," she said, "I'll work from Gramps's house tomorrow. After leaving him with Bonita for this long, I'd like to give him a break."

"That's fine." His tone was level.

She glanced at him, saw his set jaw and the stiff squared shoulders. He was upset.

Whether he was upset that he'd missed the chance to drink, or that she wanted to work from home, or some other thing, she couldn't let it govern her actions. Couldn't let herself be affected by him.

She watched the bare trees as they drove along, Fisk driving just a little too fast. Nemo panted in the back seat, bolt upright rather than lying down as he usually did.

This day had turned out to be a rough one, all around.

Lauren was able to keep the week's work with Fisk fairly impersonal, and by Saturday, they were back to a comfortable, if distant, professional relationship. Today was a big day, though; Fisk was going to do a demonstration of how to make a rocking horse in the vendors' market, just as Lauren had suggested when they'd first started working together.

As they walked into the old building that housed the market, all the sensations of Christmas overwhelmed Lauren. Classic carols over the loudspeaker conflicted with a trio of young girls belting out more modern Christmas tunes. The fragrance of evergreens and candles mingled with the sweet scents of hot chocolate and cookies. Both main aisles buzzed with activity as vendors set up their wares, everything from Christmas dish towels to full-size metal reindeer to hand-painted wooden toys. The place was way busier and more crowded than it had been when they'd stopped in before, and the public wasn't even here yet. This was just the organizers and the vendors.

Several people came up to them immediately, friends who wanted to greet one or the other of them and one staff member in an orange vest, who pointed out Fisk's designated booth.

Fisk carried in a heavy load of wood and tools with every appearance of ease. Though it was cold out, he wasn't wearing an overcoat, just his usual flannel shirt. The rolled-up sleeves showcased his muscular forearms, and Lauren's heart rate quickened. She was a sucker for a pair of brawny forearms.

Lauren wasn't the only woman eyeing Fisk up. Several craftswomen paused in their work to watch him walking toward his booth.

Be professional. Her goal today was to be an efficient office manager for Fisk's business, but to stay distant from him personally. She had to, due to his alcoholism, which she'd seen clearly the day they'd visited with his parents.

He hadn't taken a drink, but he probably would have without her interference. She'd dived into the codependent caregiver role so readily. It had felt so natural.

That was scary.

Having been told a lot of people wore Christmas clothes, Lauren had put on a red sweater and a Santa hat along with her favorite jeans. Some of the workers had taken it further, Lauren realized as customers started pouring into the building. She spotted a Mrs. Claus with a white wig and body padding, a grouchy-looking Grinch, and several female elves.

One of the elves wore an extremely short, flared green dress, sheer dark stockings and short, high-heeled boots. A green Santa hat tilted rakishly over one eye. With a start, Lauren recognized her. "Tonya? Hi!"

"How's it going?" Tonya came over. "Are you a floater, too?"

Lauren shook her head. "I'm helping Fisk," she said. As yet, he didn't need any help, but she hoped to hand out lots of business cards and take after-Christmas orders.

She and Tonya strolled down the line of vendor stalls, chatting and checking out the wares.

"Yeah, I think I'm the only floater, actually." Tonya twisted a strand of long, blond hair. "Nobody wants me in their booth all day."

"Why?" Lauren had been studying a table of ceramic Christmas earrings, but when she heard Tonya's troubled tone, she returned her attention to the other woman.

Tonya shrugged. "I'm not exactly well-liked after I started dating the guy who jilted Kelly Walsh. She's super popular, and people thought I stole her man, which I didn't."

"You're still dating him?"

Tonya shook her head. "No, that was short-term. Like most of my relationships." She lifted her hands, palms up. "To be fair, I haven't always been real nice. To people I dated or anyone else."

"You've been nice to me," Lauren said.

Tonya smiled at her. "And you've been nice to me. I appreciate that."

"Did you miss the memo that this is a family event?" A woman from the yarn craft booth next door looked Tonya up and down. "You're not exactly kid-friendly in that outfit."

Tonya's cheeks reddened. "*I* don't dress for kids," she said, looking pointedly at the yarn craft woman's bright sweater featuring a reindeer with a blinking red nose.

"No, you dress for..." The woman broke off and pressed her lips together. "Never mind. You ladies have a nice day, now."

Lauren tugged at Tonya's arm. "Come on," she said, "you can work in our booth."

Both Tonya and the yarn craft woman looked shocked.

"I can?" Tonya asked.

"Yes. We need you." Lauren led Tonya back toward Fisk's booth.

When they got there, customers were already gathering around to look at samples of Fisk's work. She let Fisk know that Tonya would be helping out, and he raised an eyebrow, but didn't object.

Lauren quickly realized that Tonya needed to be the one giving out business cards and inviting people to see Fisk work. As soon as she took on the job, more dads and grandpas came by.

Lauren took down names and explained the project in layman's terms. Fisk was making a rocking horse, an old-fashioned kind, targeted for young children. "You can order them for next year, or for a child's birthday," she explained to a small group who'd stopped by. "But if there's interest, Fisk may be leading some woodworking classes, and this could be a project. Write your names down here if you want to get on our mailing list. We'll have more information after the holidays."

Fisk's brother Alec came in, head and shoulders above most of the other people. "You sure drew a crowd, bro," he said to Fisk.

Fisk grinned and nodded at Lauren and Tonya. "It's my elves," he said.

Lauren smiled at him. It was good to see him in his element, working with wood, talking and joking with friendly people, his dog nearby.

Things got busy for a while, but when traffic slowed down, the three of them—Lauren, Fisk and Tonya—sat down and took a break. Olivia, one of the women who'd triple-teamed Lauren at the diner, was carrying around a tray of hot chocolate samples, which they all sipped appreciatively.

"I think my outfit caused a few people to gossip," Tonya said. "I hope it didn't hurt your business."

Fisk waved a hand. "They would've gossiped regardless," he said, "since I made such a fool of myself here last year."

"They get two for the price of one at this booth," Tonya joked.

"Good thing we have Lauren with her perfect reputation." Fisk raised an eyebrow at her.

Oh, if you only knew.

Gramps came by with Bonita, as they'd planned earlier. He looked tired and admitted he wasn't staying, that he'd just come to drop Bonita off.

"I'm asking too much of him," Lauren fretted after he left. "Babysitting Bonita all the time is taking it out of him."

"Might be a good idea for him to have a checkup," Fisk said.

"I've suggested that, but he doesn't want to. Doesn't like doctors." She turned to Fisk. "Could *you* maybe look at him?"

"If I can get him to agree to it," Fisk said, "but I'm not licensed or up-to-date. I'd rather try to coax him to see a real doctor."

"I couldn't talk him into it. But maybe someone outside the family, like you, would be more convincing."

"A *man*." Tonya rolled her eyes. "Want me to hold the baby?"

"Sure." Lauren handed Bonita to Tonya, who clapped her hands and laughed.

Tonya bounced her gently. "I'm not big on babies," she said to Lauren and Fisk, "but this one's a cutie."

"She is." Fisk held up wooden blocks from a set he'd put on display, and Bonita grabbed at them joyously.

Music still played, and the Santa at the end of the row of vendors boomed out a "ho-ho-ho" to a group of passing kids. Someone handed out samples of warm cinnamon muffins. Gusts of wind rattled the windows, but inside the building, all was safe and festive.

This was what Lauren wanted for Bonita. A lively, small-town event. A lively small town, period.

Then, a little bit later, she heard people talking in the next booth, and her ideal vision of small-town life deflated a bit.

Two people had moved to a spot they probably believed was more private, in the back of their booth. But the partition between their booth and Fisk's was just a piece of cloth.

"Did you see my neighbor?" a woman asked.

"Wilkins?" The man who'd said it let out a snort. "Which one is that, anyway?"

"The *alcoholic*," the woman said with an almost gleeful emphasis.

"Like I said…which one?" The man laughed and the woman joined in.

Fisk kept working, head down, a dark flush visible on his neck. So he'd heard. Lauren walked to the front of their booth, not wanting to embarrass Fisk with sympathy. She didn't know what to say, how to help without making the problem worse. She felt indignant for him, protective. Should she confront the gossips?

And then the solution appeared in the form of Fisk's brothers. They were joking around with a jewelry maker down the aisle.

"Watch the shop," she said to Tonya. "Cam! Alec! Hey!"

They turned and walked toward her, meeting her in the aisle in front of Fisk's booth and the one next door. She gave the brothers a meaningful look and nodded sideways toward the booth from which the comments about the Wilkins boys had come. "These people had some questions about your family," she said.

Both men seemed to take in the situation at a glance: Fisk, head down, working with an impassive face, and a guilty-looking couple pretending to be busy in the booth next door.

"Did you folks have something you wanted to ask us?" Cam's body was relaxed, fists unclenched, yet somehow, there was a bit of the fighter in his stance.

"We were just saying it's hard to tell you apart!" The woman giggled nervously.

Alec beckoned to Fisk. "Hey. C'mere."

Lauren watched him, half cringing. She hadn't meant to create a confrontation he didn't want. And from the way he sighed, she could tell he didn't want it.

But he walked over toward his brothers, Nemo beside him.

The three men stood in a formidable row. Cam and Alec's arms were crossed. Fisk's hands were on his hips.

Behind Lauren, Tonya let out a little sigh. "Whoa. They always were some good-looking men."

Lauren couldn't disagree.

"I'm Alec, the oldest." Alec looked steadily at the gossip. "That's Cam. And that's Fisk."

Fisk lifted a hand. "I'm the alcoholic," he said helpfully.

"Any other questions?" Alec asked.

"No!" The woman's face turned eggplant purple, and the man cleared his throat and got very busy moving boxes.

Their little group moved over to Fisk's area, and soon, the tone of the noise around them changed: people were packing away supplies and gathering coats and bags. Today, the market was only open until 1 p.m.

"Why don't you all come over for hot chocolate and tree decorating?" Alec asked, looking at Fisk. "Cam's coming. The kids would all like to see Uncle Fisk and Nemo." He turned to Lauren and Tonya. "You'd be welcome, too," he said.

"Uh, I'm going to have to take a rain check," Tonya said. "I don't actually think your wife would welcome me."

"Why not—" Lauren started to say.

"You would be—" Alec said at the same time.

Tonya waved a hand. "It's fine," she said, cutting them both off. "I'm changing, but that doesn't make my past go away. I was nasty to your wife, and I don't want to push it by crashing her home." Tonya waved and left before anyone could argue. Moments later, Fisk's brothers left, too, after repeating the invitation to join in the family gathering.

"Well, how about it?" Fisk didn't look at her as he started putting his tools away. "Will you come? Don't feel obligated," he added quickly.

She caught a glimpse of the look in his eyes. He looked somehow…raw. This event had been hard on him. He'd come and worked cheerfully, talked to people, but there had been whispers. He'd gotten into one heated conversation while Lauren had been writing up an order. And then there were the comments made within his hearing, about the Wilkins family.

People tended to judge, and they didn't forget. She hated that. Hated that Fisk, his family and Tonya were the victims of it, in the same way that she'd been a victim of the gossips and tabloids back home.

Wasn't she doing the same thing herself, though, if she refused to do anything socially with Fisk because of his past alcoholism?

She knew she had to keep her distance. She had a special

vulnerability to alcoholics. And since she'd already spent significant time with him today, the smartest, safest thing to do would be to have him drop her off at Gramps's. She didn't need to see him laughing and being appealing with his brothers. She needed to protect her heart.

At the same time, Fisk was offering her a ticket into the social world of Holiday Point. Having playmates for Bonita—and friends for herself, like Kelly and Jodi, Fisk's brothers' wives—was an important factor in whether she'd be happy here, whether she could stay.

Plus, when she put false modesty aside, she knew that she and Bonita were good medicine for Fisk.

Could she spend time with him socially without falling prey to his charms, though?

Bonita in her lap, Lauren watched covertly as he swung supplies into his arms and carried big loads out to his truck, waving off her offer to help. His strength attracted her, but even more so, she appreciated his humility.

When he came back for one final load, she stood.

"Want me to drive you home?" he asked. "Or, the invitation to visit over at Alec and Kelly's still stands."

She thought a moment, said a five-second prayer, and then made the leap. "You know, it does sound fun," she said. "Bonita and I would love to come to your brother's house."

Fisk realized his mistake the minute he walked into Alec's house with Lauren, Nemo and Bonita.

The place was filled with happy kids and Christmas sights and sounds. Cam and Jodi and their three had gotten here just ahead of them. Kelly, seven months pregnant, knelt beside six-year-old Zinnia, helping her with some sort of craft. Alec was welcoming them in, but he quickly returned to his wife's side.

And sure, there was a complicated story behind Kelly, Alec and Zinnia. But it had all worked out well, and now they were a solid family, a growing one. Alec had never looked happier.

Cam, too, had had his share of heartbreak. But he'd come out of it stronger than ever after getting together with Jodi. His sons were now every bit as much hers as his, and they'd had a baby together. Just seeing the expression on his brother's face as he took the baby from Jodi…it told the tale of how happy he was.

Fisk helped Lauren out of her coat and hung it up along with Bonita's snowsuit. He made sure Nemo's service vest was off so that Nemo could play with Kelly's therapy dog, a rescued racing greyhound named Pokey.

As he went through the motions, though, an internal debate raged.

He wanted this, wanted what his brothers had. Wanted a family of his own. It was a longing that ran deep and word-less; it was why he'd been happy rather than upset when Di had let him know that she was unexpectedly pregnant with his child.

Maybe because he'd come from such chaos, having a solid, loving family was high on his wish list. His broth-ers were the same way.

But yet, his brothers were better men than he was. Nei-ther of them seemed to have inherited their father's pen-chant for drinking. Neither had caused any trouble in town, beyond a little teenage mischief.

They'd been unfairly tarred with the Wilkins name's black brush. They'd had to work hard to overcome prob-lems they hadn't created. While for Fisk, the Wilkins repu-tation fit. He'd done all kinds of bad things in town. Being a drunk Santa, breaking up a display at the Christmas light show...that was the tip of the iceberg. He'd been a mess in every season and had acted out accordingly.

And what he'd done in Holiday Point wasn't all. He'd done worse things back in Baltimore, far worse. He didn't deserve what his brothers had. If the thought depressed him, well, he did deserve that.

His nephew JJ was trying mightily to hang a popcorn string on the Christmas tree, but between munching on it and being a little guy, he wasn't having much success. He grabbed onto a branch and nearly knocked the tree over.

Fisk took two giant steps toward the tree and lifted JJ up to where he could properly hang the popcorn string. "Thanks, Uncle Fisk," the little boy said, giving him a quick hug and then struggling to get down.

Fisk set him down and watched him rush distractedly away from his tree decorating to pick up Mork, his mother's emotional support dog. He carried the little yorkie into the kitchen, and Fisk turned to see how he could help the other kids with their decorating.

That was why he was here. To help his brothers and nieces and nephews celebrate the season. If it caused him a little ache around the heart, he could stand it. He'd gotten through worse.

He just had to remember that he *wasn't* here to be Lauren's boyfriend. Beautiful and magnetic as she was, she was out of reach for him. She deserved so much better.

Fortunately, she headed straight into the kitchen when Kelly did, and he soon heard them laughing together. He liked that about her: she was a friendly person. She wasn't judgmental, either; she even seemed to be befriending Tonya Mitford, who had few or no female friends. Lauren wasn't threatened by Tonya's tight clothes and mouthy attitude; she seemed to take the other woman in stride, seemed to see beneath Tonya's facade to the hurting person underneath. Fisk liked that about Lauren, liked it a lot.

As the men and kids decorated the big tree and a second small one, Kelly kept bringing out snacks. Cookies, because she was an expert baker with a side hustle of making Christmas cookies for everyone in town, and hot chocolate with peppermint-stick stirrers. They all munched and sipped and decorated, and Fisk felt his shoulders relax.

No, he couldn't have a family of his own, but he was fortunate to have brothers who understood him and looked beyond his faults. He needed to focus on gratitude. He did have a lot to be thankful for.

Nemo played with Kelly's greyhound and then gave in to the other dog's essential laziness. Both napped by the fire until little Mork came rushing in, sans vest, barking and pawing at them. The yorkie mix was about the size of the other two dogs' heads, but he had energy enough for all three of them. The kids got permission to tie Christmas ribbons around each dog's neck, and then Jodi started taking photos of everything for her blog.

Finally, the trees were decorated and the kids were tired. Kelly served up a tasty meal of chili and cornbread, and afterwards, the kids piled on the couch to watch a Christmas movie while the adults sat around the table, drinking coffee and nibbling on cookies and talking.

"Who'd have thought," Cam said, "that the Wilkins boys would be having a wholesome, zero-alcohol Christmas gathering and actually enjoying it?"

"We should photograph that," Jodi said promptly, and she jumped up and took a few more photos.

"You men deserve a good Christmas," Kelly said. "I know things weren't always so great when you were growing up. And Fisk, I'm so glad you've, well…" She broke off, her cheeks reddening. "So glad you're here," she finished.

Fisk could guess exactly what she'd been going to say: that she was glad he was here sober rather than intoxicated. He didn't hold it against her. "Believe me, I'm glad, too," Fisk said, smiling at her. Kelly had been there last year to see his Christmas shenanigans, and she'd still welcomed him into her family's Christmas gathering. That was part of what had helped him make his decision to quit drinking, and he was grateful to her.

Jodi must have understood the subtext, too. "If you don't mind my asking, is it hard not to be drinking? Not that you have to talk about it, if you don't want to, or…" She broke off, too, looking at Lauren. "Sorry! I'm always blurting things out. Fisk, your story is yours to tell."

"It's okay," Fisk said. "Lauren knows I have a drinking problem. In fact, she saved me when Dad pressured me to drink earlier this week."

There were exclamations all around, and questions, and Fisk explained how Dad had poured him a big shot and waved it in his face. Just the memory of it made his stomach tighten. His father had nearly caused him a major setback.

But that was wrong: he shouldn't blame it on Dad. What he did was his own responsibility. At the same time, he appreciated the assist from Lauren. "If Lauren hadn't intervened, I very well might have taken that drink," he said.

Lauren's face went pink and she waved off her role. "I felt like I had to step in, but who knows if that was the right decision. You probably would have turned down the drink on your own."

"I can't believe your dad did that," Kelly said, sounding indignant.

Fisk, Alec and Cam exchanged glances. None of them

were at all surprised. Their father had encouraged their negative behaviors. He'd supplied Fisk with his first drink at the age of twelve and had laughed when Fisk had choked on the whiskey.

Fisk had turned that into a reason to sample more whiskey until he could down it with a straight face.

"Dad was always hardest on you," Alec said. "Wish I'd stepped in more than I did."

Now it was Fisk's turn to wave off the comment. "I think Dad knew he had an easy target in me. He knows I'm like him, with the tendency to drink, anyway."

"You're like him in other ways, too," Cam said thoughtfully. "Dad could have been an artist, too, if he'd been able to stick to anything."

"That's true," Alec said. "He's real good at drawing. Maybe that's why he resents you, because you're actually making a career of your art."

"I'm not an artist," Fisk said. "I haven't done any drawing or painting in years."

They all stared at him, his brothers, their wives and Lauren.

"What?" he asked, confused.

"You're totally an artist," Jodi said. "Your work is amazing. The carvings, the lines, the personalization of all your work…you're incredibly creative."

Lauren was nodding. "Definitely an artist."

Fisk's face heated and he brushed aside their kind words. "I'm a carpenter, at most." He turned to Lauren. "Enough about the Wilkins family and our issues. I'm sure you're sick of hearing about my family."

"Yeah, tell us about your background," Cam chimed in. "Did you have big holiday celebrations yourself?"

Lauren frowned, and too late, Fisk remembered that

Lauren didn't seem to enjoy talking about her family and her background.

"My mom liked to throw big Christmas parties," she said, her voice noncommittal but somehow communicating that she didn't want to share more details. "As for me, I like a smaller, family celebration."

"Is that what you did with Bonita's dad? Oops," Jodi said. "Sorry, that was nosy. Let me just…pass around these rolls one last time."

She did, and everyone started passing dishes around even though they were all too stuffed to eat more. There was a kind of hanging silence, though; Fisk was pretty sure that everyone was still listening to see if Lauren would respond to Jodi's question.

Lauren must have realized that people were waiting. Her forehead wrinkled. "I…well, I don't actually talk about Bonita's dad a whole lot."

That was an understatement, but Fisk could understand why Lauren didn't talk about the man.

Fisk rarely mentioned Di and Scarlett, either. He and Lauren were about even in keeping their pasts to themselves.

A ball rolled their way, from the other kids, and Lauren grabbed it, obviously grateful for the distraction. She showed it to Bonita, rolled it, then set Bonita on the floor.

Bonita sank onto all fours and crawled rapidly after the ball.

"Tell us about the kids' Christmas activities," Fisk said, looking at Jodi and Kelly. He knew from experience that a way to change the subject was to get parents talking about their kids. His brothers and their wives were no exception. They immediately launched into stories about Christmas parties and pageants.

Fisk scooted his chair a little closer to Lauren's in a show of support, and she didn't move away. Instead, she smiled up at him. "Thanks," she whispered.

Emotion washed over him. He squeezed her shoulder, quick and gentle.

Alec and Kelly started clearing dishes, and Jodi refreshed everyone's drinks. The conversation got general, interrupted by a lot of "Mom!" and "Dad!" from his tired, overstimulated nieces and nephews.

Fisk's heart nearly overflowed with wanting this. The clingy kids, the eye-rolls with a sympathetic spouse, the quick kiss or arm squeeze.

Not just with anyone. With Lauren.

Nemo came over and leaned against him, whining a little. Good dog. Good to distract him.

Fisk wanted what his brothers had so badly that he could almost taste it, but he couldn't have it. He'd ruined lives back in Baltimore, and no way, no *way,* would he ruin lives here. Especially Lauren's.

Lauren was beautiful and down-to-earth. She was kind. A truly good person. She'd obviously been through a lot in her life, but it hadn't turned her bitter. It had made her more thoughtful and understanding, as far as he could see.

He cared about her too much.

He also knew his own limits. He was getting into an emotional no-man's land, and he knew where that could lead.

One of the tenets of AA was to get far, far away from temptation. He couldn't get too close to a shot of whiskey without wanting it, without being at risk of taking it. The same held true for Lauren. He needed to keep a safe distance.

When they finally all stood and started cleaning up, Fisk

took Cam aside. "Any way you could run Lauren home?" he asked.

"Sure, of course, but why don't you take her? Things are winding down here. Jodi and I will stay and help with cleanup." Cam studied him, curiosity in his eyes.

Fisk couldn't really explain. "I need to get out of here. Need to get away from her."

"How come?" Cam asked.

Fisk spread his hands. "She's like alcohol to me. Forbidden fruit."

"Does she have to be forbidden?"

Fisk looked across the room at her. She stood talking with Cam's older son, Hector. Or rather, listening as Hector eagerly explained the train set they were setting up beneath their own Christmas tree.

She would be a great mother. Already was. If only he could make a baby with her, or a bunch of them. He'd love to have a big family with her.

He couldn't. And right now, he couldn't stand it. He was getting to a bad place mentally, a place that was dangerous for him to go. Even Nemo seemed to think so, because he looked up at Fisk and pawed his leg.

"If you've got Lauren and Bonita, I'm outta here," he said to Cam. "I'll put the baby's car seat on the porch."

"Well, okay, if you're sure—"

"Later," Fisk said, and headed out into the blustery evening, running like a coward because that was all he could do.

Chapter Eight

Lauren was extremely annoyed the next afternoon when they arrived at a local nursing home.

"They" being she, Bonita, Gramps, Nemo…and Fisk.

She'd agreed to go with Gramps to the nursing home to visit with his friends. He claimed Bonita's presence would cheer up the residents and explained that several people from the church were going for a Christmas party today.

She'd figured helping others might get her out of her bad mood, which she'd been wallowing in courtesy of Fisk. What kind of guy invited you to a party—*his* family party—and then abandoned you there?

She'd hoped that visiting the nursing home would give her a much-needed break from her handsome, exasperating employer.

But here he was, driving them there in his truck.

It was true, the nursing home was on a hilly country road. It was true that snow was falling, with more predicted. She would have hesitated to take her own car out in this weather.

Still, when he stood ready to help her out of the truck, she ignored his hand and climbed down herself, Bonita in one arm, grabbing the edge of the door at the last minute to keep from falling.

She straightened, embarrassed, and tried to pull herself

together. Gramps was already headed toward the building, eager to get out of the snow and see his friends. Including one special friend, she was guessing; he was still wearing his churchgoing clothes, dress pants and a white button-down shirt, and he'd added a colorful bow tie and enough cologne to fumigate Fisk's truck.

"Can I carry something for you?" Fisk asked.

"Stop being nice," she gritted out. "I'm mad at you. I wish you hadn't come."

It had been so embarrassing last night when she'd realized her ride, Fisk, the person she'd come with, had left without her. His brother Cam had been nothing but kind when he'd driven her and Bonita home, but still. How mortifying to have to depend on someone she barely knew, because she'd been abandoned by Fisk.

He was still standing beside her, looking humble and handsome and ready to help, and it infuriated her. "You could have just loaned Gramps the truck," she said. "You didn't have to insert yourself into our plans."

"My grandmother lives here," he said mildly. "I intended to come all along, but I was planning to come alone until your grandfather called me."

"Oh." She hadn't known that his grandmother lived there, nor that Gramps had requested the ride. But it didn't excuse Fisk's behavior last night. She marched toward the door, Bonita on her hip, a diaper bag over her shoulder, and a plate of anger-baked Christmas cookies in her hands.

When she started to slip on the slick walkway, Fisk caught her by the elbow and then took the cookies from her. "I can help. You don't have to talk to me, but I don't want you and Bonita to fall."

"Fih! Fih!" Bonita said her version of his name joyously.

Lauren turned a little so that her baby was blocked from

the handsome man at her side. Petty of her, but she didn't want her unsuspecting child to fall prey to his charm, any more than she already had.

She planned to ignore Fisk, push him away and forget about him.

Inside, the big recreation room was decorated with wreaths and tabletop gingerbread houses. A tall, heavily decorated Christmas tree stood in the middle of the conference room. Someone was pounding out carols on the piano, and a group of residents, some standing and some in wheelchairs, sang along with hearty enthusiasm. Looking more closely, Lauren realized that it was Kelly's friend Olivia at the piano.

Beside Fisk, Nemo barked, calling attention to them. Fisk and Nemo were soon surrounded by residents and people from church.

After Lauren got Bonita out of her snowsuit, she straightened her outfit and walked with her across the room, bending sideways to accommodate Bonita's stiff-legged, new-toddler gait. Everyone stopped to exclaim over how cute she was, and to admire her outfit: red-and-pink striped leggings and a red dress with pink trim. "She looks like a Christmas elf!" one of the ladies said.

"Look at that bow!" one man said. Lauren had affixed a pink-and-red headband, topped by a colorful bow, on Bonita's head.

"Bah! Bah!" Bonita patted the bow on her own head, smiling at the man who'd noticed it. She was a flirt in the making, for sure.

Normally, Lauren loved showing her baby off and meeting elders with interesting stories. Today, though, her mood stayed dark.

And she needed to get ahold of herself, because these

nice people didn't need a sour-faced visitor. So she made an excuse—she had to put out her cookies—grabbed them, and turned in the opposite direction. Fortunately, she spotted Kelly. She headed toward her.

"You look ready to beat someone up with that cookie tray," Kelly said, taking it from her and putting it on a table with other refreshments. She peeled back the plastic wrap. "Those look good. I didn't know you baked."

"When I can't sleep," Lauren said.

Kelly cocked her head to one side. "Any particular reason?"

Lauren let out a disgusted breath. "You might have noticed, Fisk abandoned us at your house last night. Fortunately, Cam was able to take us home, but it still made me mad."

"Yeah, I did notice." Kelly rested her hands on her baby bump. "What was that all about?"

"I have no idea."

A young teen whom Lauren had met in the church nursery came over. "Can I take Bonita around? Lots of people would love to meet her."

"Lindsay's terrific," Kelly reassured her, and so Lauren relinquished the baby.

"Come over here and talk." Kelly gestured toward a secluded corner where a couple of chairs were set up beside a large manger scene and partially shielded by it.

"I'm supposed to be socializing." Lauren really didn't want a pep talk from Kelly about how great Fisk was.

Kelly giggled. "Nobody's going to want to socialize with you when you look so peeved," she said. "Come on, talk to me about what's got you down."

Feeling sulky, Lauren sat down beside Kelly and accepted a brownie from the plateful Kelly had snagged along the way. "Mmm. These are good. Thanks."

"Chocolate for the win," Kelly said. "I'm loving the opportunity to eat extra without feeling bad about it. Being pregnant is awesome in that regard."

"How are you feeling?" Lauren took another bite.

"I'm good. I mean, I'm seven months along, and I feel like a whale. But at least Alec's a big, tall guy. He can still pick me up and carry me."

"Impressive," Lauren said, thinking how nice it must be to have a husband who still wanted to pick up and carry his pregnant wife. Pregnancy had been the final straw in her marriage. Her ex had actively avoided her the moment she'd started to show.

"So, getting back to Fisk." Kelly took a delicate bite of brownie. "He abandoned you at my house and you're hurt."

"I'm *mad,*" Lauren corrected, and then immediately realized Kelly was right. "But hurt, too."

"Did he explain what happened?"

Lauren lifted a shoulder. "Said he got overwhelmed."

Kelly nodded. "He's pretty new to recovery. And we were talking some about his family background, which can be sort of painful for all of them. They have one other brother, Frank, who hasn't been home in years because he can't deal with his parents and his family's history around here."

"Yeah?" Lauren drew in a deep breath and let it out slowly. Kelly was trying to be kind, and Lauren needed to reciprocate. "I understand feeling upset about your past. I guess I'm mad at myself for agreeing to do anything with him, when he's so unreliable."

Kelly looked troubled, like she wanted to say more. But then Lindsay stopped by, bouncing Bonita on her hip. "Hey, I wanted to let you know that I'm starting to babysit," she said. "If you ever need a sitter, I hope you'll think of me. I can put my number in your phone."

"Okay, sure." The girl seemed a little young, but Lauren admired her initiative. And it was clear that Bonita liked her.

"I could babysit tonight or anytime," the girl, Lindsay, continued. "I know your gramps. If you don't trust me alone, I could be like a grandpa's helper while he's there."

"That's a good idea. I'd like to give him a little more of a break than he's been getting."

They exchanged phone numbers. "Okay if I keep her a little longer?" Lindsay asked.

Given Bonita's happy smile, Lauren couldn't say no, and the two of them ambled off.

Kelly picked up the thread of their conversation. "Honestly, I'd be mad, too. When I first met Alec, I always felt like he was disrespecting me, because he dated my completely gorgeous sister before he dated me. I always felt inferior."

That was surprising. Kelly seemed to have it all together, to have everything she could possibly want.

"So," Kelly continued, "is there something in your past that makes it hard for you to trust Fisk?"

Lauren lifted her hands, palms up. "He's untrustworthy! He abandoned us."

As she said the words, though, the truth crashed over her. "Just like," she said slowly, "just like my ex-husband was always abandoning me. He didn't like to take me places because it cramped his style. If we did go to a party together, half the time he'd take off with his friends and leave me stranded."

"Ugh. That must have been awful." Kelly frowned. "Did you feel like Fisk left you stranded, too?"

"I mean…not exactly. He arranged for Cam to take us home, but I was embarrassed."

Kelly nodded. "I get that. Even though Cam was fine with it I'm sure, right?"

"He was," Lauren admitted.

"And the rest of us, we know what Fisk has gone through, so we cut him some slack. But that doesn't mean you should have to do that, too."

Lauren reached for another brownie and then pulled her hand back. "Listen," she said, "I appreciate your efforts to help me understand Fisk, but it's not going to work. Me and Fisk aren't going to work."

Kelly spread her hands, shrugged and stood. "I'll leave you to figure that out." She walked away just as Fisk approached from the other direction, wheeling a silver-haired woman toward them.

Why, why, Lord? Lauren stood, but not quickly enough; Fisk and the woman reached them, and of course, Lauren couldn't be rude and walk away.

"I wanted to meet you," the woman said cheerfully, holding out a thin hand. "I keep hearing about the new girl in town who's helping my Fiscus get his business straightened out."

Lauren perched on the edge of her chair to be at the same level as the woman in the wheelchair. "It's nice to meet you. I'm guessing you're Fisk's grandma."

"You can call me Grammy Alice," she said, "and I'm very proud of him for how well he's doing."

Are you proud he takes a guest to a party and then ditches them?

Even as she had the thought, Lauren realized she was overreacting to what had happened. Probably, like Kelly had suggested, because of her own past, not because of anything Fisk had done. After all, he'd arranged for her to have a ride and he'd texted within the hour with an apology.

"Fiscus hasn't had an easy time of it," Grammy Alice said.

Lauren tilted her head to one side and looked at Fisk. "So how come you go by Fisk, not Fiscus?"

He rolled his eyes. "Don't much like my full name."

"It's a name that started as a mistake, but God doesn't make mistakes," Grammy Alice said. "His mama looked at a plant at the hospital and asked what it was called, and then named her baby after it."

"Only thing is," Fisk said, "she got the wrong information. It was a *Ficus* plant, but she heard Fiscus and that's what's on my birth certificate."

"It's unique, just like you are," his grandmother said.

"Thanks, Grammy." He kissed her cheek and sat down beside her.

"He's a soldier and an artist," Grammy said to Lauren. "A rare combination. And I do believe he likes you."

"Grammy!" Fisk's cheeks reddened. "Of course I like Lauren. She's helping me get organized, which even you have to admit is not my strength."

"That's good. You're a good team."

Gramps came over, now carrying Bonita. He pulled up another chair, and soon the two elders were reminiscing, with broad matchmaking hints tossed at Fisk and Lauren whenever they tried to leave.

Lauren half listened, thinking. She wanted love, the kind of love that Kelly seemed to have with Alec, and Jodi with Cam. But she couldn't trust her feelings for Fisk. He appealed to her for all the wrong reasons.

Finally, the event started winding down, and Lauren gratefully left the little group and went to help clean up.

Fisk came over as Lauren was getting Bonita into her snowsuit. Gramps was dressed to go, too, but kept getting waylaid by friends.

"So, I did a thing," Fisk said.

"Really?" Lauren was still annoyed with him, but less so now that she'd realized she was blaming him for more than he'd done, due to her background with her husband.

"I heard you'd talked with Lindsay about babysitting Bonita. So... I hired her to babysit tonight."

"What?" Lauren froze, her hands on the zipper of Bonita's snowsuit, and she stared at him.

"Can I take you to dinner to make up for leaving you alone at my brother's yesterday?"

She blew out a breath, adjusted Bonita's hat and then glared at Fisk. "That's totally manipulative. You can't just get a babysitter for my kid without consulting me. And to assume I'd say yes..."

He held up a hand. "I admit I overstepped. But I'm not assuming you'll say yes. If you don't want to go, it's fine. My apology can be a night to yourself. You can hole up in your room and read a book, or go out with your friends, knowing your baby is well taken care of."

That *did* sound nice. Lauren was blessed to have Gramps's assistance with Bonita, but because she needed him to take care of the baby while she was working, she rarely asked it of him at any other time. As a result, she was with Bonita for all of her nonworking moments.

"I can cancel," Fisk went on, "but I really hope you'll at least accept the sitter. And maybe also the dinner. No strings or obligations. There's a nice restaurant in Uniontown that everyone's been talking about, high-end Italian. I'd love to take you there."

Lauren studied him, frowning.

What should she do?

She found her own coat and slipped it on, shifting Bonita

from one arm to the other. Of course, Fisk helped her. His hand, when it touched her neck, felt warm and reassuring.

When he got called away to help lift some tables, she pondered his offer.

It would be nice, very nice, to have a night free of responsibility. It would be even nicer to go out to dinner with an attractive, good man. She hadn't been on a date in years.

But she knew she was susceptible to someone like Fisk for all the wrong reasons.

On the other hand, should he have to pay forever for his sins? Was she really so unforgiving that she couldn't handle having to get a ride home from a spontaneous party with someone other than him, someone he'd arranged to take her? Was she going to hold a grudge about it?

He came over. "What do you think?"

She opened her mouth to say she wouldn't go. Wisdom dictated that. So did discretion. All the qualities she wanted to have.

"I'd be happy to go," she said instead. "What time would you like to pick me up?"

Fisk had counseled himself to be friendly and neutral and distant when he walked into Gramps Tucker's house to pick Lauren up. He'd waited until the teen babysitter, Lindsay, had arrived, and then an additional few minutes for Lauren to offer instructions.

Despite his plan to keep it cool, he couldn't wait long. He knocked on the door.

Lauren answered, and he sucked in his breath.

They'd agreed to go casual, and she was…kind of. She wore a red sweater and slim black pants. Her hair was loose around her shoulders. She wore practical boots, but they were furry and cute.

"You look nice," he managed.

She smiled a little. "Come on in. I was just talking with Lindsay." As he shucked his heavy coat, she raised an eyebrow. "You look nice, too."

Fisk was glad he'd decided, at the last minute, to put on his sports coat, the only dress-up item he owned.

Lindsay was on the couch, cooing over Bonita.

"Your grandfather is home?" Fisk asked. He felt responsible; after all, he was the one who'd hired Lindsay.

"He's upstairs watching TV," Lauren explained. "I think he was happy to get a night to himself."

"You know who you look like, Lauren?" Lindsay pulled out her phone. "Like Jeff Ranier's wife."

"Who's Jeff Ranier?" Fisk asked, only half listening. He was too busy trying to calm his reaction to Lauren's beauty.

Then he realized that Lauren had gone still and white. What was *that* all about?

"He's this jerk, well, he *used* to be a big star on the country music scene, but…"

"It's time for us to go," Lauren interrupted. "And I'd like for you to feed Bonita right away. And no screens for her, okay? Babies aren't supposed to get into screen time until they're at least eighteen months."

"Of course!" Lindsay stood and shoved her phone into her pocket. "You two have a great time."

"Call me if you need anything," Lauren said. "Anything at all."

"I will, but I'll ask your grandfather first. I'm sure it'll be fine. Bonita is a great baby, aren't you?" Lindsay bounced her gently, and Bonita laughed and grabbed at Lindsay's necklace.

Fisk thought about Lauren's reaction as he shepherded

her out to the truck and drove to Uniontown, mostly as a way to stop obsessing about how pretty she was.

There was some kind of issue in Lauren's past. She'd overreacted to Lindsay's comment about that country singer, and she still seemed jumpy.

Maybe tonight, he'd learn more about her, find out what had happened to her to make her so private and closed off.

But instead of digging into her past, he ended up just enjoying his time with her. They listened to an oldies station during the thirty-minute drive to the restaurant, both singing along. The restaurant was upscale but fun, more crowded than you'd expect on a Sunday night, but Fisk had fortunately thought to make a reservation.

He hadn't done it in a long time, but he did remember how to romance a woman.

They took their time eating and shared a dessert at Fisk's insistence—chocolate, of course—and Fisk took care of the bill despite her offer to help pay.

As they walked outside, he realized he didn't want the date to end. It was still early. "Want to walk along the river path for a little while?" he asked. "If it's too cold…"

"I'm a mountain girl. I'm fine." She held out one perfect leg, showing off her furry boots, and pulled a cap out of her jacket pocket. "No mittens, but I have good pockets."

"I can keep one of your hands warm," he said, and took her hand in his.

She glanced over, but didn't pull away, and Fisk felt like pumping his arm in triumph. Instead, he cautioned himself to stay calm and cool. He just gave her hand a gentle squeeze and guided her to the trail beside the river.

The moon came out from behind a cloud, making the snow sparkle and the river shine with a silvery light. Fisk sucked in a breath of cold air and tried to concentrate on the pine trees and oaks along the path, the lonely sound of a bird, the light traffic noise in the distance.

But it was hard to concentrate on anything, holding her hand. No matter how much he reminded himself that this couldn't go anywhere, it felt like it *was* going somewhere.

"I'd like to hear more about you. You mentioned your husband and his problems, but what else was important in your life before Holiday Point?"

"Oh, well…" She trailed off. "Nothing that interesting."

Fisk was disappointed that she was holding back. But he'd respect her wishes because he understood. "I get trying to keep the past in the past. It's just, sometimes the past comes out and bites you."

"That's true."

They walked for several minutes without speaking. Their breath made clouds in the air, and a gust of wind blew Lauren's hair across her face.

He really wanted to push it back for her. He wanted to know if her hair was as soft and silky as it looked.

She glanced over and frowned. Very slightly, but he knew because he was studying her so closely.

He looked away and shot up a prayer: *Lord, You know my feelings and You know the future and the past. Guide me, please.*

"So how about you?" she asked suddenly. "What happened to cause you to start drinking?"

He snorted. "Way to turn the tables. I deserve that, I guess."

"And you're welcome to say you don't want to talk about it, like I did."

Well. Telling her all about what had happened back in Baltimore would certainly destroy the romance between them. Maybe it was God's guidance. Confession was supposed to be good for the soul, and it was also good for dousing feelings of excitement and longing. Especially when the confession was ugly, like Fisk's was.

There was a bench up ahead, and he gestured to it. "If it's dry, we can sit down."

"Sure." They did, hands still clasped.

He squeezed her hand and then pulled his away. There was no good way to start, so he just blurted out his first thought: "I had a baby."

She waited, eyes steady on his face.

He forced himself to go on. "She was just Bonita's age when she died."

This was where people usually shut down. Either that or got extremely nosy.

Lauren did neither. "Oh, Fisk. I'm so, so sorry." She closed her eyes for a moment, shaking her head. "Wow."

"Thanks." He leaned forward, propping his forearms on his thighs, staring off at the river. Ever flowing, ever changing. But some things were like that cluster of trash and branches trapped along one shoreline. They got stuck and stayed.

"What was she like?" Lauren asked, her voice quiet.

He lifted an eyebrow and looked sideways at her. "That's not what people usually ask."

She shrugged. "It's what I would want to talk about if… God forbid, I can't even imagine losing Bonita. But I feel like I'd want to keep every memory I had of her alive."

That was it, exactly. "Sometimes I avoid talking about her. Most of the time. But I never see anyone who knew her, not these days, and I'm afraid…" He broke off. What kind of a father would admit he was afraid of forgetting his own child?

A bad kind of father. Like his own. Like *him*.

"She hated wearing clothes," he said.

Lauren let out a surprised laugh. "She *did*?"

"Yep. I can't tell you how many shoes and socks I lost just walking her through the grocery store. If she could get off her shirt or dress, she'd do it in a heartbeat."

"That must have been awkward," Lauren said, laughing.

"Talk about awkward. And she burped so loud, people would stop and stare."

Lauren clapped her hand to her mouth. "Bonita used to do that, too. Even in church! Once the minister stopped preaching."

"Scarlett woke up our neighbor, and he had a hearing impairment."

She chuckled. "Tell me more about her."

"And she was strong. She could climb out of her crib. She'd just learned to do that when…" He trailed off, his smile fading. He swallowed hard. "That's why I don't talk about her much. Too emotional." His throat tightened to the point that it hurt.

She reached over and rubbed his back, gently. "That has to be so hard," she said quietly. "So, so hard."

He nodded, shutting his eyes to hold back the tears that wanted to come out. But when he closed his eyes, it was as if he could see Scarlett there, burping and climbing and laughing. Pulling off her shoes and tossing them to the floor.

Things she'd never get to do again.

He let his head sink into his hands and took deep breaths.

Could he have saved her, if he'd made a better decision on that awful day?

Lauren kept rubbing his back, gently. The human touch grounded him. After a while, he started to notice the cold wind that chilled his neck, the distant sound of a diesel truck on the highway.

He opened his eyes, lifted his head and looked over at Lauren. "Sorry. You got more of a story than you bargained for."

She shook her head. "I'd like to hear more, if you still want to talk about her. Did you live with Scarlett full-time?"

He couldn't believe she wanted to go on hearing about this, but telling her did feel good somehow. "More and more," he said. "Her mom and I weren't married. I know that's not ideal, but it was just a part of a pretty bad lifestyle I was living." He leaned back and looked up at the sky, part sparkling with stars, the other part covered with clouds. The moon peeked out from behind a cloud, then was covered over again. "We tried living together," he went on, "but honestly, we didn't get along very well. Still, I was hoping to try again. Having a baby slowed me down. Made me think about what was important."

"I know the feeling," she said quietly. She'd stopped rubbing his back, but her hand still rested there, lightly.

"You do, don't you?"

She nodded, but didn't go into her own story. "I'm so sorry you lost her," she said. "Words can't really help, but I am truly sorry for what you went through."

"Do you want to know what happened, how she died?"

"Do you want to tell me?"

Did he? He was an emotional wreck just from talking a little about Scarlett. "Maybe not tonight," he said. And immediately, he felt his own cowardice. He was supposed to be pushing her away with an ugly truth, not making her sympathetic to him.

"If you ever want to talk about her, or about what happened, I'm here to listen," she said.

She wasn't saying that losing Scarlett was God's will. She wasn't telling Fisk to get over it. She was just willing to listen, and appreciation for her kindness and goodness swept over him.

She was too kind and good for the likes of him, but right now…he really, really wanted to hold her. He craved her arms around him.

In the distance, a car door slammed. Voices spoke, laughed and then faded away.

Lauren moved her hand from his back to touch his arm. "Are you okay?"

He put his hand over hers. "I am. Kind of."

"Good." She scooted closer and hugged him.

The feel of her arms around him healed something deep inside, and feelings welled up in him. He hugged her back. Brushed her hair away from her face, and yes, it *was* as soft as it had looked.

Her eyes looked huge as she gazed at him steadily.

He leaned closer. She didn't move away.

And then all of a sudden, he was kissing her.

Chapter Nine

Lauren had never felt anything that could remotely compare to kissing Fisk.

His lips on hers were warm, his touch gentle and restrained. Beneath the restraint, she felt his passion. He was a man of high emotions. He'd proven it tonight.

Maybe he was just seeking relief from all the feelings. Maybe that was why he'd kissed her.

She pulled back and looked into his eyes. "Feel better?" she asked, letting a smile cross her face.

He smiled back at her. "I feel great. Except I don't want to stop. You're incredible." He lowered his lips to hers again and kissed her more deeply.

Electricity crackled through her body. No longer was she aware of the cold air around them, the pine trees rustling in the wind, the icy scent of snow. She was only aware of him, this wonderful, creative, hurting man who for whatever reason, seemed to want to be close to her.

He made a little sound in his throat, a kind of growl, and she recognized it for what it was: passion, not pain.

A warning bell seemed to ring, very quietly, but persistently. There was a reason she needed to keep some distance from Fisk. There was a reason to be wary of the intense desire to wrap her arms around him more tightly, to get closer, as close as she could.

She let her fingers fork through his hair and inhaled the clean, woodsy scent of him. She felt the acceleration in his breathing, the beating of his heart. She wanted to turn off her brain. To feel, to be swept off her feet.

She wanted that, but she was an adult. She had self-control.

She forced herself to pull away.

He didn't seem to want to let go.

"Fisk," she whispered. Why was she whispering? "Fisk, we'd better get back."

He tilted his head to one side and studied her, his eyes aflame with such intensity that she pulled away. That seemed to bring him back to an awareness of their surroundings and their situation. "We do have responsibilities, don't we?"

She nodded. "I hate to say it, but yes."

He stood and drew her to her feet, and then hugged her gently, kissed her on the forehead, and let her go.

Without talking, they walked hand in hand to Fisk's truck. He put some kind of classical music on. "Sit closer," he invited, and she scooted to the middle seat.

His strong body warmed her as they drove over the mountain roads and back through Holiday Point. They passed the spot where they'd met, and she remembered how he'd sunk down into the snow when he'd heard Bonita cry.

Now, she understood. And she felt for him, deeply.

Was there any chance this connection between them could grow?

Her skeptical side doubted it, but oh, she wanted to believe that something could come of it, that somehow, love could flourish between them.

* * *

The next morning, Fisk stood outside his house, throwing a ball for Nemo and watching the dog frolic in the new snow.

Lauren was already in the shop. He'd seen her coming and, like a coward, had waited to take Nemo outside until she had time to settle in the building.

The sky was blue, the air still and cold, the snow sparkling. A beautiful winter day.

Fisk felt horrible.

Just do it, he told himself.

He'd tossed and turned all night, his mind full of Lauren's beauty and her kiss, on the one hand, and then of the day he'd lost Scarlett and Di.

In the wee hours, he'd come to a decision.

No matter how sweet and lovely Lauren was—in fact, *because* of how sweet and lovely she was—he had to push her away. That would be easy: he just had to tell her the truth, the whole truth, about his past.

Nemo trotted up, tongue hanging out, legs matted with icy balls of snow, and he realized he'd been standing here too long without a coat. Rather than going inside his house to grab one, he marched toward the shop.

He had to do this before he gave in to his weaker wants and needs.

As soon as he walked in, his eyes found her. And oh, no. She was smiling at him, a warm, *we-have-a-secret* smile.

He wanted more than anything to walk over to the office area and kiss her, to hold her in his arms, to lose his doubts in the softness and sweetness of her. Moreover, the way she was looking at him, she'd welcome his embrace.

No.

Instead of heading over to her desk right away as he

usually did, to joke around and grab coffee and talk about the day's priorities, he went right to his workspace. He had to pull himself together before he did what he had to do.

Grabbing any old project—an antique washboard someone wanted him to refinish—he sat down and tried to do mindless hand sanding.

Nemo nudged at him. Maybe telling him he was off his routine. Maybe sensing his internal turmoil. "Lie down," he ordered.

Nemo complied, head on paws, eyes fixed on Fisk.

He kept sanding, but from the corner of his eye he could see her. That green sweater fit her well and, he was sure, set off her eyes.

Her gorgeous eyes were the last thing he should be thinking about. He should be planning out his speech. But he kept hearing her hum along with the Christmas playlist. Kept remembering the light perfume she'd worn last night, how it had tickled his nose when he'd kissed her neck.

Kissing her had been one of the best experiences of his life. He remembered every sound she'd made, how her hair had felt, all soft, how her lips had tasted.

"Hey."

He looked up and she was standing there, and yes, her sweater did bring out the beauty of her eyes. He wasn't a painter, but he'd sure give a try to painting her.

"Um, here's a list of projects for you to work on today. We need to move along Gramps's project and finish the bench for Mrs. Sanford. If you can get started on the coffee table for Elton and Bertha Johnson, all the better."

He opened his mouth and no response came out. He snapped it shut.

The phone buzzed behind her and she handed him the list of projects and went back over to her desk. He heard her answering someone's question about a woodworking class—"That's a great idea, I'll talk to Fisk about gift certificates!"—and reassuring someone else that their cabinet would be complete by the beginning of next week.

He needed to stop paying attention to Lauren and start paying attention to his work. He set the washboard aside and picked up the corner cupboard Lauren's grandfather had commissioned. He looked it over, feeling for rough spots, sanding a couple of them down. He needed to get a coat of stain on it today. He definitely didn't want to let Gramps down; the man was a friend and had been a big help to Fisk. Even though he'd understand if his project was late, that didn't mean Fisk wanted to slack off.

He needed to rebuild his reputation in this town, or rather, to build a good reputation. It started with people close to him.

He started to open the can of wood stain and then the sound of Lauren's voice, talking to yet another person on the phone, sent him back to dreaming about last night. She'd been so warm toward him. The surprise of that had filled him with joy.

Nemo barked, and Fisk realized he'd gone still.

No way was he going to get any work done until he'd had his talk with her. He ran a hand down Nemo's back for courage and walked over, the dog trotting alongside him.

"When you can get a break," he said, "we need to talk."

"Okay," she said, her expression wary. She turned down the ringer on her phone. "What's up?"

He pulled a stool over and sat down, her desk a barrier between them.

She was studying him with compassion and warmth, and he tried to memorize that expression. This was the last time she'd look at him fondly. The last time she'd think of him as a potential partner.

Talk.

"I didn't tell you the whole story last night," he began.

There was a pounding on the shop door, and then it opened. Gramps Tucker and Bonita came in.

Relief. He didn't have to spoil everything with Lauren, not quite yet. He walked over to greet the older man, taking the baby from his arms.

Lauren came over, too, and started unzipping Bonita's snowsuit, her closeness making Fisk sweat. "Do you need me to take her for the rest of the day?" she asked her grandfather.

"No, this is just a quick visit." Gramps unzipped his jacket, but left it on. "I just wanted to check on that corner cupboard."

"Come on over," Fisk said. He handed the baby to Lauren and guided Gramps over to where he'd been about to get to work on staining the cupboard.

"Oh, that's nice. Beautiful. You'll have it done by the weekend?"

"Absolutely."

Gramps studied him. "You doing okay?"

"Sure," he said.

Gramps looked over at Lauren. "You're both skittish this morning," he said.

Fisk looked at Lauren, and their eyes locked. Her face went pink.

"We're just real busy," Fisk said, "trying to knock out the last of the Christmas orders."

"I'll leave you to it, then," Gramps said. He took Bonita from Lauren, waved away her repeated offer to keep the baby here, and trudged out, his shoulders ramrod straight.

"He's lonely," Lauren said.

Fisk nodded, thinking that he should do more to help Gramps, keep him company.

After all, he himself would one day be an old man alone. He should try to learn the ropes from Gramps. He'd take Gramps to a hockey game up in Pittsburgh. No need to even dream of using the tickets he had been given to take Lauren to it.

"Well, I guess I'll get back to work. Unless…you wanted to talk to me?"

Tell her.

He followed her back to her desk and sat back down. "Look," he said, "I can't be in a relationship."

Blunt. Clumsy. But his words would do the job.

She studied his face for a long moment. Then, "Can I ask why?"

He picked up a pencil and tapped the eraser end on the desk, then flipped it and tapped the pointed end. Over and over. Finally, he stopped and met her eyes. "Like I said, I left some things out when I told you about, about Scarlett, last night."

She nodded. "Okay. What did you leave out?"

He sucked in a breath and launched into the story. How he'd confronted Di's group of friends and told them that neither he nor Di would be hanging out with them anymore, and that Di wouldn't be buying any more recreational drugs from them, nor selling them.

"Did you know she was using and selling drugs?" Lauren asked.

"Using, yes, I figured that out pretty quickly," he said. "Selling, I only learned about when some lowlifes came to her apartment when I was there. Scarlett was there too, of course. I blew up and sent them packing and laid into her,

made her tell me her source and how long she'd been selling. It wasn't that long, so I figured it would be easy to get
her out of it. Crucial, too, because I didn't want Scarlett
around those people."

"How did she react?"

He shrugged. "She was mad. Of course. She'd been
caught, and she wasn't going to get to keep making money
doing what she wanted to do." He looked at his hands. "As
it turned out, she didn't get to do it, or anything else. Never
again."

"You lost her, too?"

He nodded.

"Oh, Fisk. I'm sorry."

He waved away her sympathy. "I handled it all wrong.
I thought I was going to stay in Baltimore and protect her
from those guys, when I should have looked for a way to
leave town. How hard is that to do? I could have brought
them here."

Lauren swallowed. "It's a good place to hide."

That was an odd thing to say. But he didn't pursue it, because he needed to get out the rest of the terrible story. "I
was walking away from Di's lowlife friends when Di came
squealing up. She had Scarlett in the front seat, no car seat."

Lauren let out an "oh" that sounded like a sigh. "So that's
why you were intent that Bonita use the car seat, even for
a short drive," she said.

"What? Oh. Yeah." She was talking about the first time
they'd met. "Anyway, her so-called friends started shooting. The car crashed into the corner of a building, and I
could see…" His throat tightened. "It was bad. I was pretty
sure that neither of them survived the crash. I took off after
the shooters."

Lauren's brow wrinkled and she crossed her arms as if to hold herself together. "How awful."

"That's right. It was awful. I was awful. Because…" He looked down at his knees. "I heard the baby crying, but I kept running after those men who'd done it."

"You…heard your baby crying?"

He nodded. "I think so."

"And you kept running?"

"I did."

The lights on the phone flashed, but she ignored them.

He pushed himself to continue talking, to show her what a horrible man he was and why he couldn't be with her, even though he wanted it with all his heart. "I abandoned them, Lauren. When I'd knocked one of the dealers down and the police came and took over, I ran back, but it was too late. They were both gone."

He remembered the sound of the sirens, the police on their walkie-talkies, the murmurs and shouts of the crowd. He remembered arriving at the car at the same moment as the EMTs did. Wrenching the doors open together. And then…blood and death and despair.

Nemo jumped his paws up onto Fisk's leg and he ran his hands over the dog, not looking at Lauren, not wanting to see the disgust and horror that had to be on her face.

"I just have one question for you," she said.

"I'll answer anything." He stole a glance at her and didn't see the disgust he expected. Instead, her head was tilted to one side, her eyes compassionate.

She didn't speak for a moment, and then, "Were you drinking?"

He closed his eyes. Of course, that was her question. She had a history with alcoholics.

Although the sympathy he'd seen on her face gave him

an absurd boost of hope, he didn't deserve sympathy. Didn't deserve *her*.

Telling her he'd been drinking would push her away, for real and for good.

He thought back to that day, before everything had gone down. He didn't drink much back then. But, considering it had been a Saturday night, it was likely he'd had a beer.

Yes. He was pretty sure he'd had one earlier that day.

"Fisk?"

He swallowed hard and sealed his fate. "Yes," he said, "I'd been drinking."

Lauren stayed the rest of the day, managing Fisk's business, doing her job. She even communicated with Fisk about a change in Loreli Lenox's garden bench and a new order for a houseful of cabinets. Communicated pleasantly. But only because she kept reminding herself: *It's a job, he's the boss, there's nothing personal here.*

That was a hard thing to keep in mind. She'd been stupid and started to care about Fisk, and then she'd learned the uglier details about his past. She didn't entirely understand what had happened—Fisk had sounded a little fuzzy about it all—but she knew two things: he'd failed to care for his child when she'd needed it, and he'd been drinking. And that, right there, was the problem.

Her own reaction to his revelations raised a red flag. Her fatal attraction to alcoholics had kicked in again, and even now, she kept excusing his behavior to herself. *Survivor's guilt makes people blame themselves for things that weren't really their fault. Probably, there was nothing he could have done. Men have those adrenaline spurts that made them automatically fight and protect rather than nurture.*

But that was just her codependency talking.

Her workday over, Lauren would have liked nothing better than to put on her flannel pajamas and crawl into bed to watch her favorite mindless TV show. But Gramps and Bonita had been in the house all day. Gramps still seemed a little depressed, and Bonita was fussy.

Lauren needed to make an effort. So they went to town and were soon walking into the park, where the annual Christmas Tree Display was going on.

The wonderland of brightly lit trees made Bonita's eyes widen. She shouted and pointed from one colorful tree to another. Gramps's weathered face creased in a smile as he looked around at the lights, and soon he was introducing Lauren and Bonita to friends and acquaintances.

Bonita went into full-on charm mode, smiling at everyone. Her green plaid Christmas headband topped with a red poinsettia looked adorable on her, giving Lauren a big burst of mama-pride. They strolled down the walkway lined with heavily decorated trees, headed toward the point where the rivers came together and where the music and bonfires were centered.

"Let's get something at the food trucks and take our dinners to eat by the fire," Lauren suggested, so they got into line for a truck featuring hot sandwiches. Pulled pork dinners in hand, they headed toward the bonfire.

Vendor stands of wreaths and yard decorations had attracted a crowd, and they wove through slowly, admiring the colorful wares. Soon a voice called out to them: Tonya, here by herself, nursing a hot chocolate as she strolled along. "Join us," Lauren suggested, and introduced her grandfather. Tonya looked happy to be included, and they settled by the fire.

Gramps and Tonya knew people in common, and they went to the same church, so they chatted happily while

Lauren got out food for Bonita: crackers and cheese cubes and thin slices of apple.

Focusing on Bonita's meal gave Lauren the chance to think, and of course, her thoughts turned to Fisk.

When they'd kissed, she'd felt an amazing connection with him, unlike anything she'd ever experienced before. She'd gotten the absurd hope that something might work between them.

You thought that because you're codependent. He's an alcoholic.

His acknowledgement that he'd been drinking when his child and girlfriend were killed had extinguished any hope that Fisk and Lauren could be together.

She wanted a safe haven for Bonita, she thought, brushing back the child's hair and adjusting her hat. But that meant she had to dump Fisk. No two ways about it. He wasn't safe. He'd allowed his own baby to die.

The very idea of that clashed with her impression of Fisk. The first time she'd met him, on the snowy road near Gramps's place, he'd come to her assistance. Yes, he'd had a meltdown, but it was because he'd heard Bonita crying and thought that Lauren looked like his late girlfriend. He was definitely a man who cared.

And yet, caring wasn't enough. You had to have the behaviors to back it up, and apparently, Fisk didn't. Carelessness, mistakes and damage, sometimes severe damage, were typical of a drinker. She'd experienced similar— though not anything as bad as what had happened to Fisk's family—with both her husband and her father. The alcoholic's need for a drink superseded any love they had for friends and family.

What Fisk had done, making the wrong decision, ignoring his baby's cries, was typical of an alcoholic. Not that they always meant harm, but they certainly caused it.

I want love, a sad voice inside her said, making her clench her fists like a child in tantrum mode. She wanted love, and she wanted love with Fisk. She genuinely liked him and enjoyed spending time with him, talking with him.

As for finding him attractive? That had been the case from the beginning.

But she couldn't let her thoughts go in that direction. She needed to concentrate on what she had, the family she had, Gramps and Bonita. She pulled herself out of her own spiraling thoughts and refocused her attention on them. She pulled out a board book for Bonita, who cuddled in Lauren's lap in her warm coat, paging through it.

Tonya seemed happy to get to know them all better and was especially intrigued by their family. Which made sense, given what she'd heard about Tonya's neglected upbringing.

She wrapped her arms around her knees, sitting on the blanket they'd brought and placed near one of the bonfires. "You seem so close," she said to Gramps and Lauren. "Have you always been?"

Lauren glanced at Gramps, then reached over and squeezed his calloused hand. "I've been close with him since I was a little kid. He's always been there for me."

"Nothing made me happier," he said, smiling at her. "And now that we have this little beauty, it's even better." He rubbed Bonita's back.

Bonita looked up at him, grabbed his weathered hand and tugged it to her mouth. She started gnawing on his finger.

"Bonita! No chewing Gramps." Lauren dug around in her bag and found a teething toy shaped like a strawberry. She handed it to Bonita.

"This one can chew on my fingers any time she wants," said Gramps. He clicked his tongue at Bonita, making her laugh.

The sight warmed Lauren's heart. The close relationship developing between Bonita and Gramps made moving to Holiday Point feel like a great decision.

"What about the generation in between the two of you?" Tonya asked, looking from Lauren to Gramps. "Is your dad, or your mom, close to the family as well?"

Again, Lauren glanced at Gramps. "I'm his daughter's child. And my mom was sort of close to Gramps, I guess. Wasn't she? At one time?"

"We were close until she started scrapping with her mother. That was when she was a teenager and making not the best choices in boys she dated. Of course, I sided with my wife, but that seemed to push Lauren's mother into some very inappropriate men's arms."

"Including my dad's," Lauren said ruefully.

"You don't get along with your dad? Is he living?" Tonya seemed somehow hungry for the answers.

Lauren didn't want to dive into the details of her father's decline and death. "My dad passed away three years ago," she said, keeping it simple.

"And her mom bounced right into another man's arms," Gramps said. "This one painted himself as some kind of European royalty, which I made the mistake of expressing doubt about. She hasn't spoken to me since."

"Oh, that's so sad," Tonya said. "Do you speak with your mom?" she asked Lauren.

"I speak to her when I get the chance," she said. "Mom is living overseas with her new husband, and there's just not much opportunity for us to talk."

"Gosh, that stinks," Tonya said. "I always feel sorry for

myself because my parents were…how do I say it…not the most devoted. I envy families who are close, but I guess looks can be deceiving."

"I feel fortunate to be close with Gramps." Lauren leaned over and gave Gramps a sideways hug. "Tell us about your family, Tonya."

Tonya waved a hand. "Another time. I've had a nice evening with you all, and I don't want to ruin it." She gave a little smile, and Lauren resolved to ask her about her family another time. From what Tonya and Fisk had discussed earlier, things hadn't been good, and Tonya just might need to talk about it. And she didn't seem to have a whole lot of friends.

Their time together had successfully distracted Lauren from her feelings about Fisk, but they came rushing back when Tonya said, "Oh, wow," and gestured toward a couple of men, clinging onto each other and staggering. People were veering away from them, picking up their curious kids.

Lauren squinted. Was that Fisk?

It was. Fisk and another man, older. It looked like his father.

Gramps got to his feet. "I'll go see if there's anything I can do to help," he said.

"No need," Tonya said. "There's his brother."

"Alec will help them." Lauren turned away. She didn't want to watch this go down. She'd hoped, after he'd turned down the drink at his parents' house, that he would rededicate himself to his sobriety. Apparently, that hadn't happened.

More evidence that she needed to stay far, far away from him.

Lauren lifted Bonita, now yawning and rubbing her

eyes, and held her against her shoulder, rocking her gently. It was as much for her own comfort as for Bonita's.

She couldn't believe Fisk had gone straight back into drinking after telling her about his past mistakes. What would happen next? Would he descend into a full-on binge? Was she about to have to make a bunch of phone calls to his customers, telling them he couldn't deliver after all?

Chapter Ten

Fisk tried to get his father's arm around his neck so he could support his walking, or rather, staggering.

Around them, Christmas music and lights created a festive atmosphere at odds with Fisk's current situation. As he got his father into some semblance of walking, he looked neither to the right nor the left. He didn't want to know who all was watching.

When he'd seen his father drinking at a no-alcohol community event and tipping over a Christmas tree, then apologizing in a loud, slurred voice, he'd wanted to run in the opposite direction. He was trying to rebuild his own reputation and he felt he was succeeding.

But family was family. He'd get Dad out of this crowded gathering and over to the diner for coffee and a meal.

Dad stumbled and nearly pulled Fisk over. He wasn't a heavy man, but he was tall and right now, he had no muscle control. No way was he going to make it to the street and then the half block to the diner.

Fisk caught sight of a couple of faces he knew and his own face heated. *What do I do now, Lord?*

Suddenly, some of his father's weight was off him and he was able to stand. His brother Alec was on the other side of

Dad. "Let's get him to the church's booth," he said. "They have coffee and hot chocolate and chairs."

Relieved, Fisk turned in the direction Alec indicated. They supported their father between them and made their way to a small tent with a simple cross on the front.

"You got him?" Alec was looking across the crowd. "I left Kelly and Zinnia back at the food tent, and I really don't want them to come looking for me and see Dad like this."

"Lemme see my granddaughter," Dad slurred out.

"Not tonight, Dad," Fisk said, and turned to Alec. "You go on. I've got this." He didn't love it, but Fisk was the right person for this job. He was way too familiar with a drunk's behavior and motivations, having been there himself not that long ago. And he didn't have kids or a wife to worry about.

And he wouldn't. He'd had a glimmer of hope when he'd kissed Lauren, but he'd snuffed it out immediately. He didn't deserve a wife and child, not after what had happened. Didn't deserve Lauren.

He'd seen her earlier tonight, walking around with Bonita and Gramps Tucker, and longing had hit him right in the gut.

Now, he only hoped she hadn't seen him and his father.

The pastor himself was manning the booth, and he brought two cups of coffee over. "Thanks," Fisk said. "Okay if Dad and I sit here for a little while?"

"Of course. That's what we're here for. Hi, Mr. Wilkins. I'm Pastor Mike Stone. It's good to meet you after hearing so much about you."

Dad guffawed. "People talk about me all the time. Don't know why. My good looksssh?"

"That's probably it." The pastor smiled and looked at Fisk. "Would you like for me to pray with you?"

"Absolutely," Fisk said. He and the pastor bowed their heads and the man said a quiet prayer. Fisk tried to focus on it, but he could hear Dad fumbling in the pockets of his heavy coat. Something clinked, and when Fisk looked over, he saw that Dad had pulled out a bottle of whiskey.

"Put it away," he told his father. "Not acceptable in a family gathering."

"But itssss Fireball. Your fav'rite."

"Not legal in the park," the pastor said. "Let me get you a sandwich."

"Put the bottle away or give it to me to pitch," Fisk ordered.

Dad put the bottle into an inner pocket of his coat, then ate the proffered sandwich and chugged his coffee. Good.

"Thanks for the food and coffee," Fisk said to the pastor, meaning it. Not every religious leader would get their hands dirty with a drunk. "This has been a big help. I think it's best I try to get him home now. Maybe he can come to church with me one of these days."

He wanted to talk to Dad about AA. Even more, he wanted to talk to him about Christ. If Fisk couldn't have a family of his own, at least he could help his family of origin. It would be good for Dad, and really good for Mom, to get them both into a better lifestyle and a faith community.

But now wasn't the time. Any insights Dad had, any commitments he made, would be forgotten once he'd sobered up. "Let's go home, Dad," he said. He turned down the preacher's offer of help and walked with his father toward High Street, steadying him when he staggered. At least Dad was able to stand upright now, mostly.

Fisk headed toward his truck, but Dad had other ideas. "Lesss get a drink," he said. "Buy you one."

A surprise jolt of temptation rocked Fisk. If he wasn't going to escape his past or his reputation, why not hit the bar?

Dad fumbled for his flask and held it out. "One for the road," he said.

Fisk had enjoyed a few epic drinking sessions with his father. In a way, it was the closest they'd ever been. Drinking, problem drinking, was what they had in common.

Dad opened the flask, and the cinnamon smell of the whiskey tickled Fisk's nose. Wow, did that ever smell good. He started to reach for the flask.

Walk away from temptation. The words of his AA sponsor echoed in his mind, backed up by that verse from first Corinthians, something about how God wouldn't tempt you beyond what you could bear.

Fisk wasn't sure he could bear this temptation, especially when he glanced around and saw several acquaintances watching him and his father.

What was the rest of that verse? There was more to it. Something about how he'd provide a way to escape temptation if you needed it.

Would He, though?

Fisk looked around at the families and lit-up trees and the live nativity at the entrance to the park. Then he looked at his father, holding out the flask.

Which did he choose?

He blew out a breath and took a step back, leaving his father to balance on his own. "Put it away, Dad. I'm taking you home."

"Buzzkiller." Dad took a swig and then pocketed his flask.

"Truck's over this way." He nodded toward the parking lot and then took Dad's elbow and guided him to it.

He was grateful Lauren wasn't here to see this mess.

As he closed the passenger door and then strode around to the driver's side, though, he spotted Gramps Tucker, Lauren and Bonita. They were headed toward the on-street parking. Maybe they hadn't seen Dad and Fisk.

What did it matter, though, if they did? If she did?

But it did matter. He got his father into his truck, climbed in himself and started it up. He steered past the crowd and sped up as he turned the corner, intent on getting out of here.

And then he heard a sickening, familiar sound.

A police siren. And the flashing red and blue lights to go with it.

Naturally, the officer was someone Fisk had gone to school with. Someone who surely knew Fisk's reputation as well as that of the whole Wilkins family.

"Are you aware of why I stopped you?" the man asked.

Fisk was pretty sure he knew the real reason. But in his experience, it was best to say as little as possible to the cops. "No, sir."

"Can I see your license and registration?" the officer asked, not acknowledging that he knew Fisk.

That was okay, because Fisk couldn't remember the guy's name, either. Mitchell? Martin? Fisk reached across his muttering father and got the required documents out of the glove box. He handed them to the officer, who glanced over them.

A small crowd was gathering. Dad's mutterings turned into curses. Loud ones. Of course.

"Mr. Wilkins," the officer said to Fisk. "Are you aware that you're required to use a signal when making a turn?"

Fisk blew out a breath. "Yes, sir." Of all the stupid things to mess up, and only because he was trying to run away from an audience for Wilkins family drama. Now, that audience would grow bigger.

He knew the stop wasn't really about the turn signal, though. That was an excuse to find out if he was intoxicated. People must have seen him and Dad getting into the car and called the cops. Maybe the officer himself had spotted them staggering.

Officer Maxwell—that was it—leaned closer and sniffed. "Have you been drinking?"

"No, sir," Fisk said promptly.

"Any use of controlled substances?"

"No, sir." Fisk was thankful for the military training that made respectful responses automatic. He certainly hadn't learned them at his father's knee.

Maxwell flashed a light inside the car. Fisk glanced over and nearly groaned aloud. Dad's flask of Fireball sat right on the console between the seats, lid off. When had Dad done that, and why on earth hadn't he put it away? Why hadn't Fisk *thrown* it away the moment he'd seen it, before Dad had ever gotten in the truck?

"I'm gonna ask you to please exit the vehicle."

Fisk drew in a breath and offered up a quick prayer for patience and help. Then he opened the door and climbed down, moving slowly so as not to make the officer nervous. From inside the truck, Dad's curses continued to ring out.

Fisk couldn't help looking around. More of a crowd was gathering, pulling their coats tighter around themselves, their breath making clouds in the cold air.

"Step over this way." The officer gestured Fisk closer. "I'm going to do a couple of field sobriety tests."

Thankfully, they were shielded from the main part of the crowd by the officer's SUV, but Fisk's face still burned. The man did the standard light-in-the-eyes procedure and the stand-on-one-leg test. Fisk had done both before. Funny how much easier they were to do when you were completely sober. Fisk had never driven drunk, never tested above the legal limit, but he'd nudged that edge a little too closely a time or two.

"See this line over here?" Maxwell beckoned him to a painted parking-space line. Unfortunately, it just happened to be in full view of the onlookers.

Fisk walked over, when really he wanted to sink into the ground and disappear. That, or disappear into a bottle. If he was going to be accused of being a drunk anyway...

"Now, I want you to put your left foot on the line, and then put your right foot in directly in front of it, heel to—"

"I know how to do the test," Fisk gritted out.

"Sir, I'm required by law to give you instructions and demonstrate the procedure," Maxwell said, and started from the beginning again.

Fisk made his face expressionless as he listened to the man's overly detailed directions. Then he performed the heel-toe walk-the-line drill perfectly.

"I told you to count the steps aloud," the officer said. "Do it again."

Was Maxwell demeaning him on purpose? Fisk's face and neck felt impossibly hot. This *couldn't* be happening.

He repeated the exercise, counting the steps.

When he came to a halt, he could see that several people in the crowd were shooing others away. Whether because they'd realized there was nothing to see, or because they were kindheartedly wanting to spare Fisk embarrassment, he didn't know, but he was thankful.

He scanned the remaining onlookers, wondering if Alec and his family were still here. No, if Alec saw this happening, he'd be front and center immediately, offering support and demanding to know what was going on.

Lauren, on the other hand... He hoped with all his heart

that she'd continued on her way and was now out of range of this particular set of humiliations.

And then he saw her, Bonita balanced on her hip, her expression unreadable. Gramps stood with his hand on her shoulder, frowning. Tonya stood beside them, pressing her lips together.

"Mr. Wilkins, I'm just going to issue you two citations. One for the open container, and one for turning without a signal."

Fisk knew what was expected of him. "Thank you, sir." It rankled to call someone younger than you were "sir," but the balance of power was all in the officer's favor right now. And he *was* grateful that he wasn't going to get a DUI charge that he'd have to defend himself against.

"You'll want to get your dad home," Maxwell said.

What do you think I was doing? "I plan to, sir." And the sooner the better, because Dad's insults were getting more vulgar and more personal now.

Fisk wiped the sweat off his forehead with his sleeve. It was a cold night, but he was hot inside. Hot with anger, and embarrassment, and misery.

His goal to restore his reputation in this town had just been shot to pieces.

The morning after the Christmas Tree event, Lauren walked across the lawn toward the shop. Her feet crunched in the inch of snow that had fallen and crusted over. Sunrise had turned the sky pink and purple, with a rim of gold illuminating the lacy branches of the trees.

She kept thinking about last night. Poor Fisk.

She'd been focused on his alcoholism after hearing his story about Baltimore. She'd seen him staggering in the park, and that feeling had been reinforced.

But when he'd been stopped—for nothing, basically—she'd felt an unwelcome rush of sympathy, especially when she'd seen the misery on his face.

Murmurs from the crowd had been sympathetic, too. People said things like "his dad's been like that forever" and "Fisk was helping his dad, not drinking" and "Maxwell was on a power trip well before he got his badge." Lauren had seen for herself that Fisk had performed the sobriety test perfectly.

Was her sympathy misplaced, or was it an appropriate and genuine feeling? That was what she needed to figure out. She'd done a couple of short video sessions with her therapist since arriving in Holiday Point, talking about how to handle her codependence, and she probably needed to do another one. Because whatever her feelings for Fisk meant, they weren't going away. They were growing.

Maybe talking with him today would help her understand herself.

She turned the knob to walk into the shop and found it locked. Then she paid attention and realized the place was dark. She peeked in the windows to be sure: no Fisk.

Where was he? He always arrived before she did.

Had he left town? Was he sick?

Had he succumbed to the desire to drink after that embarrassing encounter with the police last night? Was he now hung over?

She tromped through the snow to the front door of Fisk's cottage. She'd never been inside before, and she didn't intend on going in now, but maybe ringing the doorbell would rouse him. She rang it, waited, rang it again. Nemo's distinctive bark rang out from somewhere inside.

She pounded on the door, but there was no response.

Had something happened to him? She tried the doorknob and found it unlocked. After a moment's hesitation, she walked inside.

She wouldn't have expected perfect housekeeping from a man who lived alone, but in fact, Fisk's place was pristine. There were no dishes in the sink or on the counters; everything was neatly stowed in beautiful glass-front cabinets. The round, thick kitchen table was fine wood, clearly Fisk's workmanship.

The living room was the same: neat and simple, with some great furniture.

And she was creepy to be looking around his house uninvited. "Fisk? You around?"

She heard Nemo's bark upstairs, and after a moment's hesitation, followed it toward its source.

Nemo's tail thumped loudly and he hurried to greet her at the door of the first bedroom she came to. At the same time, she heard a groan.

She sucked in a breath and walked in, swamped by memories of helping her dad, and her husband, wake up after a bender.

Fisk sprawled in bed, eyes closed. His hair was mussed, his face stubbled.

She sniffed and didn't smell alcohol. "Fisk? Hey, wake up." Gingerly, she touched his shoulder.

He sat up abruptly, rubbing his face, looking around. When his eyes rested on her, they went darker.

Her own face heated. "You didn't show up at the shop, so I came to find you."

He drew in a breath, heaved it out in a sigh and patted the bed. For a minute, Lauren thought he meant for her to sit down. But then Nemo jumped up, and Fisk rubbed the dog's sides while Nemo panted happily. Clearly, this was a

morning ritual for them, and Lauren felt like an intruder—
or maybe a privileged, close family member—to see it.

Fisk shook his head a few times and picked up his phone,
studied it. "Whoa. I slept through my alarm. That never
happens." He blinked at it and frowned.

"Lots of messages?" she asked.

"Yeah." His voice had turned bleak. Obviously, he'd just
remembered what had gone down last night.

And this setting was way, way too intimate. She backed
toward the door. "You need to get down to the shop and get
to work," she said, hearing the gruffness of her own voice.
She scurried down the stairs and out, needing to get far, far
away from the all-too-appealing sight of Fisk waking up.

Twenty minutes later, Lauren had settled down and was
at least attempting to work. Fisk came into the shop, dressed
in his usual T-shirt and jeans, hair damp. He left the door
between his cottage and the shop open. "Nemo's eating his
breakfast. Sorry I wasn't here. Thanks for waking me up."
He didn't look her in the eye.

It was just as well, because she was still struggling to
manage her reaction to him—a complex mixture of attraction and sympathy and concern. She busied herself fixing
him a cup of coffee, which she handed to him along with
a spoon and the jug of creamer.

"Thanks." He doctored his coffee and took a gulp. "I
didn't expect to see you here after that fiasco last night.
Figured you'd quit."

"I wouldn't leave you in the lurch like that."

He shrugged. "I'm guessing a lot of people will cancel
their orders. Things will slow down."

"Actually," she said as she studied her computer screen,
"you have three new orders."

"What?" He set down his coffee and came to look over her shoulder.

He didn't touch her. He never did, at work. But she still felt his heat, close behind her. She drew in a slow breath and let it out, trying to stay calm and professional.

"I don't get it," he said.

"People don't blame you for your dad," she said, and then looked away. She had, at first. "Did you look at your phone?"

He shook his head and pulled it out of his back pocket. "It's full of messages, but I'm not sure I want to read them."

"If they're anything like the shop messages I just picked up, they're supportive," she assured him.

His phone buzzed. He looked at it. "It's my brother Cam. I'd better take it."

He held the phone to his ear as he walked over to his work area. "Yeah, I'm okay. No, don't come out. Go see Dad, if anything. He's gotta be pretty hungover."

He listened some more. "Yeah. Thanks. Okay, I have to get to work." He looked back at Lauren and lifted his eyebrows. "Don't I?"

She nodded and pointed at Mrs. Wittinger's project.

They worked quietly for most of the morning. They hadn't really talked about what had happened. She'd intended to express her support, but maybe it wasn't necessary. Maybe he could see it from the fact that she was here.

Toward lunchtime, there was some shouting outside. Lauren went to the window, and Fisk was close behind her.

An unfamiliar car was in Gramps's driveway, and a man on the porch, his stance aggressive.

The door opened. Gramps came out, red-faced and shouting, and the man backed quickly away, hands up.

"What's that Gramps is holding?" Lauren asked, unable to believe she was seeing.

"A rifle," Fisk said grimly. He shrugged into his coat. "You stay here."

"Are you kidding? My baby's inside!" She grabbed her jacket and followed Fisk out, shrugging into it as she jogged toward Gramps.

"Stay back," Fisk ordered.

The man who'd been shouting at Gramps jumped into his car and squealed away. They both hurried to Gramps. He was sweating, his face still red and angry.

"Come on inside," Fisk said to Gramps.

Lauren pushed past both of them and into the living room, where Bonita sat in front of her latest toy, a plastic gas station. She barely looked up when Lauren came in. Obviously, whatever had gone down with Gramps and that man, it hadn't bothered Bonita. Lauren went back into the kitchen, where Gramps sat at the table while Fisk poured him a glass of ice water.

Gramps was breathing hard. Fisk put the water in front of him. "You feeling dizzy at all? Having any pain?"

"No pain, except that jerk who I just chased away. *He* was a pain."

"What happened?" Lauren squeezed her grandfather's shoulder and then pulled out a chair across from him and sat down.

"He was asking for you," Gramps said. "Some city jerk. I didn't like his looks."

Dread snaked down Lauren's spine. Had someone from her husband's world of fame and tabloids found her? It had been bound to happen, but she wasn't ready, not in the least.

"So why'd you pull out your rifle?" Fisk asked. He was still studying Gramps.

"Scare him off. Guy like that, he's going to blow over when he feels the slightest little breeze."

"Did he identify himself?"

"Said he was a reporter. Didn't say from where."

Lauren's stomach twisted. She was glad Fisk was there, on the one hand, because he could help protect Gramps and Bonita. But what if he found out the truth? Wouldn't he want her out of his life, his employ, and his sight, immediately?

She wasn't sure, but his presence here, now, made her worry. "Go ahead back to work," she said. "You have so much to do. I'll do what I can from here and stay with Gramps, in case he needs anything."

Fisk raised an eyebrow. "You're sure you're okay?"

"Yes, I'm fine."

Fisk nodded and walked back toward the shop. Obviously, he knew he was being dismissed.

Lauren went inside with Gramps. "I can fix us some lunch in a little while," she said. "And I can take Bonita. I'm sorry you had to deal with that."

"Actually…" Gramps looked uncomfortable.

"What?"

"Do you mind taking Bonita and spending the rest of the day at the shop? Grab some lunch to take over. I picked up some things and there's extra."

She studied him, puzzled. "I can, but why?"

His ruddy face got ruddier. "I, uh, I have a lady friend coming over."

"Gramps! Who is it?"

"Go on, now. This little incident set me back. Gotta get ready. I have a cabinet to wrap."

She hadn't known Fisk had finished Gramps's cabinet. He must have done it in one of his late-night sessions. "Sure, of course! Have fun!" Lauren was half concerned, half chuckling as she gathered Bonita's things and a container of leftovers from the kitchen. She'd just ask Fisk if she could heat it up.

Then she paused. Fisk.

She'd wanted to get away from him. Instead, she and Bonita were going to spend the rest of the day with him. She just hoped he wouldn't ask too many uncomfortable questions about that reporter and her past.

Chapter Eleven

❧

Fisk had been thinking about Lauren when she showed up at the shop door, Bonita on her hip.

What had that reporter wanted? Guy seemed sleazy. Lauren had been upset out of proportion to what had happened, or so it had seemed to Fisk. Something was going on.

A city jerk, as Gramps had said, who wanted to talk to Lauren. Why? What had she been involved in?

"Can we come in?" she asked now.

He held the door for her. "Of course." He realized he meant it, too. An independent type, he liked being alone and sometimes found an unplanned visit from someone intrusive.

Not from Lauren, though. He was happy to see her, to spend time together, working or talking.

She shucked her coat and knelt to perch Bonita on one knee and unzip her pink jacket. "Gramps kicked us out," she said, frowning.

"Gah-puh," Bonita said.

"Yes, Gramps!" Lauren clapped her hands and looked at Fisk, her face pink with excitement. "That's the first time she said it so clearly."

"Nice." Fisk remembered the phase when he'd interpreted Scarlett's so-called words to others. A baby's babbling sounded like mush to the uninitiated, but a parent could make at least some sense of it.

"Gah! Gah!" Bonita pointed in the direction of Gramps Tucker's house.

"Yes, Gramps is at his house. You love Gramps!" Lauren smoothed Bonita's hair. "It's so exciting when she learns a new word."

Fisk nodded and tried to smile. But he couldn't help thinking that it was a phase Scarlett would never go through.

The idea filled him with sadness, but it wasn't unbearable. Didn't send Nemo rushing from where he lay beside Fisk's workbench, watching them.

Fisk took Bonita's jacket and hung it up. "So Gramps kicked you out? Why?"

The frown returned to Lauren's face. "Because he has a *lady friend* coming over, and he wants privacy."

"Really?" Fisk raised his eyebrows and grinned. "Way to go, Gramps Tucker!"

"Oh, stop. It's not funny." She walked toward the office area, slowly, bent a little sideways to hold Bonita's hand.

Fisk followed them. "You're right. It's not funny, it's nice."

"What if she's taking advantage?" Lauren showed Bonita a round tub of blocks and the baby plopped down, reaching for them. "I don't even know who this woman is."

Fisk went to the coffee machine and poured a cup for Lauren. "Let the man have a life."

She glared. "I don't smother him."

Bonita banged blocks on the floor, babbling at them.

"You're overprotective," Fisk said. "Gramps Tucker needs love and affection, just like anyone else." *Just like me.* The thought flashed into his mind, surprising him.

It was true, though. Now that he'd been a year sober, had started a business that looked like it would make him a fair living, he'd begun to want love and affection more. Even to think he might be able to support a family, like his brothers were doing.

"Gramps hasn't dated since Gram died. He doesn't date!"

"Maybe it's time." Fisk frowned as he handed her the cup of coffee and a small jug of Hazelnut Crème. "He's been alone for how long? About ten years?"

"Yeah." She doctored her coffee. At their feet, Bonita overturned the whole toy container, spilling colorful blocks all over the industrial rug.

Fisk knew he was getting soft when the sight of kids' blocks seemed to fit right into his shop. In fact... Bonita's were plastic, but wood ones would be way better. Maybe one for every letter of the alphabet, carved with items starting with that letter.

He stored away the new project idea in his mind. No time for it now. He needed to get to work on his current stuff.

He headed toward his workbench. When he looked back, he saw that Bonita was toddling after him and Lauren behind her.

Lauren's forehead was still wrinkled, her expression concerned. "Why can't he just, like, get a hobby or something?"

"He *has* hobbies. Connecting with other people, or one special person...that's different." Fisk had been hungry for that kind of connection, coming out of his childhood family. It had caused him to make some terrible choices. "You're not wrong to be concerned, but I think Gramps has a good head on his shoulders. He'll figure out a way to do the right thing."

"But what if he gets into a bad situation?" Lauren knelt and stopped Bonita, now on her knees, from grabbing a tray of screws.

Bonita's face screwed up and she wailed.

Nemo came over and flopped down beside her, and her crying turned to instant laughter. She grabbed Nemo's fur in her two sticky hands.

Nemo turned and licked her fingers, making her giggle.

Fisk picked up the tray of screws and put it on a shelf. "Going to have to childproof this place," he said. "She's getting more mobile and curious all the time." He pressed his lips together. How would Scarlett have been at this age?

"You know," Lauren said, obviously still thinking about her grandfather, "what if the woman he's invited over is after his money, or is into drugs, or is just mean or something?"

"All relationships aren't bad," he reminded her. "Gramps Tucker is a pretty good judge of people. He wouldn't have invited someone who's a troublemaker or a jerk. It's probably some nice lady from church."

"But he's vulnerable. Lonely." She crossed her arms over her chest and tapped her toe, fretting.

Fisk was filled with the urge to wrap his arms around her and calm her fears. He stifled it. "If he starts dating someone and it goes bad, well, he's just like the rest of us fools for love."

She opened her mouth as if to argue and then snapped it shut. She looked at him searchingly, then looked off across the shop toward the windows. Fisk would have given quite a lot to know what was going on behind those emerald-green eyes.

Whatever it was, she was unhappy about it. Which made sense; she was just coming off a divorce. Fisk needed to be more sensitive.

"Hey, I'm sorry." He took two steps toward her and put

an arm around her shoulder, gave her a quick squeeze, then stepped away. "Didn't mean to bring you down."

"It's okay. I'm just…gun-shy. From the past."

He looked into her eyes and couldn't turn away. He wanted to know everything about this woman, her childhood, her marriage, what made her laugh and what had hurt her.

Her gaze was steady, speculative.

Don't kiss her. Do not kiss her again. Fisk drew in a deep breath and let it out.

Nemo gave three sharp yips and when Fisk looked over, he saw that the dog was blocking Bonita from crawling into the power-tool area of the shop floor. She was inches away from a mounted circular saw.

"Bonita!" Lauren cried. They both rushed to her, and Lauren swept her into her arms. "No, no, Bonita! Oh my baby, I'm so sorry I didn't keep a better eye on you." She knelt beside Nemo, holding a struggling Bonita on her hip. "And you, sir, are a very good boy and you're getting half of my lunch."

"Good boy," Fisk said, kneeling too. He rubbed Nemo's sides as Lauren quieted Bonita's protests by swaying her back and forth. The dog arched and stretched his neck in pleasure.

Fisk was just going through the motions, though. Inside, he was berating himself. He'd almost let another child get into danger, possibly fatal danger. If she'd reached for the saw or flipped the wrong switch…there were safety features, sure, but there was just too much sharp, dangerous stuff over here.

He had to nip that possibility in the bud. "We're going to move furniture to make an enclosure. I don't want her on the shop floor ever again." Before Lauren could answer, he strode toward the office area and started moving book-cases and cabinets to make an enclosed square.

He hadn't walled off this area yet because he wanted to do it right: with a separate entrance and HVAC system so nobody in the office choked on dust. But a little dust was better than a child's life at risk. He jammed a book-case into place.

Lauren offered to help, holding Bonita, but he waved her off. "Just…chill a minute while I do this, and then you can eat your lunch and work here." It wasn't ideal, and Bonita would undoubtedly fuss, wanting to explore.

She'd be safe, though. That was paramount.

The other necessity was shutting himself off from Lauren. She was making him want what he couldn't have.

Fisk worked hard for the rest of the week, taking time off only to attend two AA meetings, a precautionary measure his sponsor had recommended because holidays were tough.

It was crunch time with the Christmas projects. The holiday itself was next Wednesday, and everyone wanted their items completed before Christmas Eve. With Lauren's help, he went smoothly from one project to the next. Any questions he had, about supplies or customer preferences, he told her about and she took it from there.

It was working. *She* was working out as an office manager, making an incredible difference in the business.

But she scurried off each evening when the day's work was completed. No more socializing. And yeah, maybe that had something to do with that moment in the shop, before Nemo had alerted them to Bonita's risky location. He knew in his head that he couldn't start anything up with her, but his heart hadn't gotten the memo. If not for the distraction of Bonita's safety, he might have kissed her. And from her expression, she might have let him.

Or maybe it had meant nothing to her. Maybe her rapid after-work departures had to do with Gramps Tucker, who'd apparently been stood up by the lady he'd invited to lunch. The old man seemed blue, and Fisk was glad Lauren and Bonita were there to cheer him up.

The time was coming, he feared, when he'd need cheering up himself. If he hadn't thought about it before, this week brought to his awareness how much he'd come to depend on Lauren, not just for business, but because he enjoyed having her around.

He was becoming acutely aware of what it would be like when Christmas was over. She'd probably want to find another job.

He didn't know if he could do without her—professionally or personally. Which was why he was glum as he pulled up to the park for the annual Dog Parade on Friday evening, Nemo panting on the passenger seat beside him.

Coming here wasn't his idea. His sisters-in-law were involved with planning the event, and they'd asked him to run a booth after the parade, teaching people about service dogs.

He wanted to help them out, and he wanted to be a responsible member of the community. That meant giving back, even though he felt plenty ridiculous after the fiasco with his father.

The whole town knew he and Dad had been staggering around and getting in trouble with the police. If they hadn't seen it themselves, they'd heard about it within a day or two, often exaggerated. A couple of outlandish questions from friends in town had shown him that.

Given that he'd suddenly become notorious, and not in

a good way—again—he'd offered to back out of the dog event. But Kelly and Jodi wouldn't hear of it. They'd waved away his concern, saying that the people of Holiday Point knew that he'd changed and had sympathy for his problems with his dad.

As he and Nemo headed toward the staging area for the parade, the sound of people's voices seemed to come in waves. Dying down as he approached, continuing in a low murmur as he walked by. It wasn't negative-sounding, though. He even heard a few "cute dog" and "looking good" comments.

"Look, Nemo, they're impressed with you even before you're all decked out." Kelly knelt in front of Nemo and held out a hand. He offered a paw, as he'd been taught.

An audible "awwww" went up from the surrounding spectators.

Kelly reached into her backpack and pulled out a red ribbon. She tied it around Nemo's neck. "There, what do you think? We could add a Santa hat, or there's a little vest—"

"No, a bow is fine," Fisk interrupted. He got enough flack about the fact that Nemo wasn't the hound or pit bull breed favored in the surrounding countryside. To deck him out in an elaborate costume wouldn't help Nemo build a more macho reputation.

Nemo seemed to smile up at him, panting, possibly thanking Fisk for not allowing him to be dressed up in an entire ridiculous costume. He reached down and rubbed the dog's soft ears. "Don't say I never did anything for you, buddy."

The parade went quickly since it was basically a loop around the park. Afterwards, Fisk staffed the booth about service dogs, sharing duties with Jodi, whose tiny Yorkie mix was an emotional support dog. Mork and Nemo sniffed each other and barked a little, but soon settled down on opposite sides of the long table so that each could get the maximum amount of attention from passersby.

"When he has his vest on, like now," Fisk explained to a little boy, "you can't pet or distract him unless the handler says it's okay."

"Is it okay?" The kid's eyes begged him to say yes.

"Sure. Nemo, release."

Nemo wagged his tail and approached the boy, letting out a couple of excited-sounding yips.

"Not so loud!" the kid said, holding his hands over his ears. But he was soon rubbing Nemo's sides and being licked in the face.

Fisk felt good when a recent military vet took him aside to ask about the dog's effect on PTSD. Fisk was able to say, truthfully, that Nemo had saved his sanity if not his life.

As the night went on and the crowd thinned out, Fisk spotted Lauren. She was helping at the church's booth across the way. He leaned back in his chair and tried not to be obvious about staring at her.

He was getting more glimmerings of a ridiculous idea: that he could settle down here in Holiday Point, build a life like his brothers had, start a family. He wanted it to be with her.

But every time he went a certain distance in that direction, mentally, he came up against a brick wall: the accident, and his own response to it. All he'd lost. All his girlfriend and daughter had lost. Their very lives.

It was a matter of respect to Scarlett and Di. He couldn't replace them.

"Do you want to talk about it?" Jodi asked, nudging him. "About *her*?"

"What?" Fisk started and pulled himself back into the present. "About who?"

"Whom," she said. Then grinned. "Sorry. I shouldn't be the grammar police. And I meant, do you want to talk about Lauren?"

He opened his mouth to deny any interest in the topic, but then he shut it. "Is it that obvious?"

"Yeah. It is. I saw you staring." She patted his arm. "We're all rooting for the two of you to get together."

"Is that so?" The idea that his brothers and their wives thought he could handle a relationship...that was food for thought. But then again, there was the past looming up.

His brothers had never even met Scarlet and Di. They didn't know what he'd had and lost. Oh, they knew the technical details of what had happened. But they didn't know how it felt because no one could. "Yeah. I really like Lauren. She's great. So is Bonita. But I can't replace what I lost."

"Of course not." Jodi squeezed his arm. "You'll never replace them. But if the situation were reversed, would you want Di to live alone for the rest of her life?"

Would he? "No, of course not. But that's different. She wasn't at fault, she was a victim."

"Was she, though?" Jodi asked. "Who drove into a dangerous area with a baby in the front seat, no child restraint? And who got involved with those awful drug dealers in the first place?"

Fisk blew out a breath and shook his head. "Remind me never to tell Cam anything again."

"Marital privilege," she informed him loftily. Then her face went serious. "I know you feel guilty, and no doubt you had some fault in the thing, but..." She lifted her hands, palms up. "Who hasn't done something that hurt someone else? We're all human, Fisk."

He thought about it and smiled at her. "You're pretty smart, you know? If you'd only gone out with me that time I asked you. Think of the benefits to my life." It was a family joke, that Fisk had asked Jodi out first and that Cam had nearly decked him for it. Cam's anger had upset Jodi, but it had also been the catalyst for Cam to get help and for the two of them to move forward toward a permanent commitment.

They were steady and happy now. It was a good thing. He and Jodi wouldn't have suited each other, even though he appreciated her good qualities and knew she was the best thing that had ever happened to Cam.

She snorted. "You know I like you better as a brother-in-law," she said. "But I wouldn't mind if you'd add a sister-in-law into the equation. Especially if it's Lauren."

He shook his head quickly. "Can't happen."

"People can change and be redeemed," she said. "*You* can change. You already have."

"I still feel guilty." He looked away as he spoke, his hand on Nemo's reassuring head.

"Look at me," Jodi said, and waited until he did. "That guilt is not from God," she continued. "If you're sincerely sorry and have asked for forgiveness, it'll be given."

Fisk nodded, indicating he'd think about what she'd said.

He'd asked for forgiveness. But how could you be forgiven for letting your child die?

The morning after the dog parade dawned bright and sunny. A good day to make Christmas deliveries. Lauren had enlisted Gramps to take care of Bonita, and Fisk had even left Nemo at home. They needed to focus to get a truckload of completed cabinets, benches and coffee tables into happy customers' hands and homes.

They were making good progress, Lauren thought as she backed into a tight corner of a customer's living room, holding one end of a coffee table Fisk had finished yesterday. She set her end down and stretched her sore shoulders and neck. She tried not to look at Fisk's muscular arms, bare in a T-shirt despite the cold temperatures outside.

"There," Fisk said, settling his end into position. "Got it."

"It's absolutely gorgeous!" Marie Finnegan jumped up and down, clapping her hands, frizzy white hair bouncing.

"Sorry I couldn't wait until Christmas for you to see it." Mr. Finnegan stood in the doorway, clutching it for balance. He used his cane to walk farther into the room, looking down at the coffee table with satisfaction. "It turned out just like I told you to do it." He shook Fisk's hand.

Mrs. Finnegan threw her arms around her husband. "You were listening when I told you I wanted a place to put my feet up. But this is way too beautiful to use for that!"

"All my coffee tables are made tough, ma'am," Fisk said. "You can put your feet up with no worries."

Lauren made a note on her phone. They should put that information into the shop's website. They should also get a stock of big red ribbons for occasions like this. Customers could request a delivery at a particular time when the recipient was sure to be home. Make it more clearly a gift and an event. It would be a good service for them to provide next year.

If there *was* a next year for their collaboration.

She glanced at the time. "We have to hurry off," she said to the enthusiastic elders. "We're playing Santa today to a lot of people."

As they got into the truck and headed toward their next delivery, Fisk smiled over at her. "Thanks for rescuing me. I usually end up talking to the Finnegans all day."

"Which is great. They're lovely. But today's important for your reputation as a business. People are counting on getting their things on time. Especially—"

"Don't remind me," he interrupted, holding up a hand and grinning. "Mrs. Wittinger. I know. She's called me four times since the shop closed yesterday."

"On your home phone?" Lauren's jaw dropped.

"Yep. Don't know how she got the number."

"That's harassment!"

He shrugged. "She's just anxious. Wants everything to be perfect when her daughter arrives for the holidays."

As they drove back toward Holiday Point, Lauren's chest ached. The day was gorgeous, sunny, with a few gusts of wind kicking the snow into sparkling explosions. The sky above the roadside pines was clear, deep blue.

She loved being near Fisk. She wanted their ease back. Wanted more than ease, to be honest, but she didn't dare allow it, not any of it.

Ahead, a deer leaped into the road and stood, staring at them. Fisk hit the brakes, then eased them to a stop. "Go ahead, Mama," he said, and sure enough, two smaller, white-spotted deer bounded into the roadway. Then they all disappeared into the woods.

She looked over to see Fisk smiling at the deer, and then at her. "Beautiful," he said.

His eyes lingered, and she suddenly got the feeling he was talking about more than the deer. Her cheeks warmed and she looked down at her jeans-clad knees.

He put the truck into gear and then reached over and gave her shoulder a quick squeeze. "Hey. This is hard, but we'll make it."

His touch warmed and calmed her, but what did he

mean? She shifted in her seat to face him. "What's hard, exactly?"

"Being together, doing stuff together. I just wish it could be more." He drove on as if he hadn't just dropped a small but significant bombshell.

She took a deep breath to calm her heart. "You feel it, too?"

"I do." He pulled out onto the road and drove forward. "I... I can't let it go forward, but I sure do regret it."

"I know. Me, too."

"I never want to hurt you, Lauren."

You already have. But it wasn't his fault. He couldn't help how appealing he was, especially to someone like her.

When she didn't respond, he turned on the radio to the quiet country station they both liked, and they rode into town for their next-to-last delivery. Junior Jacobs wanted his cabinet delivered to his pickup so that he could take it home and hide it from his wife until Christmas Day. Lauren focused on that, and the stark branches against a blue sky, and the quiet country music. Gradually, she settled down. For now, at least.

They parked beside Junior's pickup, right outside the hardware store where he'd said it would be. As they stood debating the best way to get the bulky garden bench out of one pickup and into the other, Lauren heard an oily voice behind her. "There you are."

She turned, and that same reporter Gramps had sent packing jammed a microphone into her face. Directly behind him, another man was filming. "How long have you been hiding out in Small Town, USA?" the reporter asked.

It was one of those questions that couldn't be answered. She held up a hand and turned away.

Fisk had been getting tools out of the back of the truck,

but now, suddenly, he was beside her. He put a protective arm around her. "What's going on?"

The man who'd been filming moved closer. Lauren kept her face turned away.

"Is this your new boyfriend? Did you know your husband is sick?"

He's my ex-husband, not my husband. "Sick?" she asked, looking at the reporter. "What's wrong with him?"

Instead of answering, he smiled in an unpleasant way. "Could be that the new charges got him down."

"New…charges." She leaned back against the truck, shaking her head as concern washed over her. She didn't love her ex-husband any longer. If, as a Christian, she could hate him, she would have. At the same time, he was the father of her beloved daughter. So his health, and his legal situation, were of interest to her.

But would she get useful information out of this particular reporter? Very doubtful.

Hearing voices, she realized for the first time that a small crowd was gathering around them. *Oh no.* If the truth about her past got out, she wouldn't be able to contain it again. Everyone here would find out who she was. Who Bonita's dad was.

This was everything she'd been trying to avoid when she'd moved here. She looked down and prayed a wordless prayer for help.

Fisk stepped in front of her, a solid physical block between her and the reporter and cameraman. "You men need to leave. Now."

"Most of those underage girls described the inside of your house and car," the so-called reporter said, and her heart lurched. It was an exaggeration, but at least a couple of the girls had been in the house or his car, she knew.

That made her feel frustrated and powerless and…defiled, somehow.

"How can you claim you didn't know?"

"I had no idea what he was doing," she choked out through a tight throat.

Several cars had pulled up and stopped. Car doors slammed. Pedestrians, blocked from moving along by the small crowd, craned their necks to watch the scene.

Someone was pushing through the crowd. "Get on out of here," Kelly said loudly as she marched up to the reporter.

Jodi, close behind her, took on the cameraman. She got within inches of his face. "You delete that footage before I take the whole camera away from you."

"Hey, hey!" The reported started backing away, clinging to the cameraman's arm. "Just looking for a story."

"Trying to earn a living," the cameraman added.

"There are better ways." Jodi propped her hands on her hips and glared at both men. "We don't like bullies here in Holiday Point. In fact, we don't tolerate them at all, so unless you can improve your game, get out."

The reporter tried to sidle past them, but then Tonya stepped out of the crowd, her thigh-high boots, sparkly sweater and long curls seeming to dazzle both men. "Come on over here," she said, gesturing them toward the diner. "I'll tell you everything you need to know."

The reporter's eyes widened and he followed her like an obedient puppy, not seeming to notice the broad wink she shot toward Lauren. The cameraman trailed after them, camera down, glancing back at Jodi as if he were afraid to video anything more.

Thank you, Lauren mouthed to Kelly and Jodi.

The crowd was dispersing, helped along by Jodi and

Kelly's repeated "nothing to see here, folks" and "don't give that kind of jerk any attention."

Lauren leaned against the tailgate of Fisk's truck, stunned, feeling warm even in the cold air. "I've been found," she said to Fisk, dazed.

"Yep." He turned and spoke to Kelly and Jodi briefly, and then everyone left except Fisk. "You want to talk about any of that?"

She shook her head. "Not this minute, when we have deliveries to make. Unless…do you want to fire me?"

"*Fire* you?"

"Because of my connection with a notorious sex offender. Fisk, he was my husband. He's Bonita's father, and he had a thing for underage girls." She'd been warm with embarrassment, but suddenly she felt cold, so cold.

Fisk tucked his coat around her shoulders. "That's horrible. It really is. But believe me, I know you can't be blamed for what other people do. Plenty of people, like my brothers, had to construct a reputation apart from me and Dad. It's not your fault."

"Do you think…" She straightened and started untying the ropes holding in the bench. "Do you think the rest of Holiday Point will agree with you? I just didn't want…" Her throat tightened. "Bonita. I didn't want her to be affected by what her father did."

"She's bound to be affected in some way." He was untying the rest of the ropes, and then they lifted the bench together. "Everyone's affected by their past and their families. But don't worry about people here."

"I do worry. How can I not? It's so awful, what he did. And I was a complete idiot. I guess it's better than my knowing what was going on and doing nothing, which is what a lot of people thought was the case. Still, stupidity is no excuse. I was wrong to be so oblivious to the fact that Jeff was hooking up with teenagers when he went on tour."

"We're all pretty forgiving here in Holiday Point. Of course, there are gossips. But most of us believe you can be made new, forgiven for any wrongs, move forward." He hoisted the bench, taking most of its weight. "That's the only way I can stay here, believe me."

They put the bench into the back of the other pickup and then Fisk steered the truck toward Mrs. Wittinger's, their last delivery.

Lauren's head was spinning. She looked down at herself. Was she still here? Was anything different?

But no; she was still herself, riding in a truck through the town she'd grown fond of, beside Fisk. She'd been discovered, and she'd survived. So far, at least.

If she'd been discovered here, she could live anywhere. So did she want to stay?

The answer came quickly as she reflected on the wonderful way people had protected her and shooed the bothersome reporter away.

She did want to be here. She loved it here.

It hurt that she couldn't have Fisk. But wouldn't it be better to be near him than not?

And the fact that he hadn't been horrified by her dark, secret history gave her the slightest glimmer of hope. Maybe, if she could get her codependency under control, something could work between them.

They were just pulling out onto Main Street when an old sedan wheezed to a stop in front of them, its horn honking.

"That's Gramps!" she said. Was something wrong? Where was Bonita?

Chapter Twelve

Fisk veered into a parking space, worried. By the time he opened his door, Gramps Tucker had pulled in beside him. He seemed alert, not upset or ill. Still, Lauren rushed to him. A moment later she had Bonita out of her car seat and was swaying with her, talking to Gramps.

The baby looked around, wide-eyed. She zeroed in on a big snowman decoration and pointed to it, babbling.

So she was fine and Gramps appeared to be fine. The only thing Fisk could think of was that Gramps had heard the reporter had come back. In a town like Holiday Point, that sort of news traveled fast.

If Gramps thought Lauren was at risk, it made all the sense in the world that he'd put Bonita into her car seat and rushed to town. Even now, Lauren was hugging him and talking with him, pointing in the direction the reporter had gone.

The crowd had died away quickly, most people returning to their busy, Saturday-before-Christmas errands, buying specialty foods and last-minute gifts at the local shops.

Jodi and Kelly approached Fisk while Lauren talked to her grandfather.

"That was wild," Kelly said. "A real paparazzi in Holiday Point! Is Lauren okay?"

"She seems fine," Fisk said, nodding toward where she was talking with her grandfather, both of them smiling. "Did someone check on Tonya?"

"She's right over there." Jodi pointed, and they all looked.

Tonya stood beside a small truck, lecturing the driver through the window.

"He looks miserable," Fisk observed.

"Like he's trying to leave and she won't let him." Jodi was laughing.

The man revved the engine, and Tonya put a hand on the vehicle's open window, shaking her head, still talking rapidly.

"Tonya's turning out to be all right," Kelly said.

Jodi stared at her. "You're amazing. I would be hard pressed to forgive the woman who started dating my ex-fiancé, like, instantly after our breakup." Apparently, that was what Tonya had done last year. It was all pretty foggy to Fisk, because he'd been drinking heavily at the time.

He breathed in the crisp, cold air and thanked God he'd been able to get out of that lifestyle.

Kelly smiled at Jodi. "It's a lot easier to forgive and forget when you're falling in love with someone else."

Falling in love. With someone else.

Was Fisk doing that, with Lauren? Honesty compelled him to admit to himself that yes, he was. It had happened quickly—the move from his initial physical attraction to something much, much deeper.

"Anyway," Kelly went on, "that was a shocker, what he said about Lauren's ex. I had no idea she was involved in some public scandal."

"She was." Jodi waved to a couple of teenage girls walking by. "I know it for a fact. But none of it was her fault."

Both Kelly and Fisk stared at Jodi. "You knew?" Kelly asked.

"I knew," Jodi said. She looked from Fisk to Kelly. "What? I'm online all the time, doing research for my blog. I'll send you a link to an unbiased article about what happened. But know this: she had nothing to do with her husband's criminal behavior."

"I could have told you that," Fisk said. "She's a good person, all the way through."

Kelly and Jodi glanced at each other. "She *is* good," Jodi said, and nudged him. "Maybe it's time you made a move."

"That's right," Kelly said. "Get on it, Fisk."

Fisk managed a wry smile. "So this is what it's like to have sisters, huh?"

"That's right." Jodi raised her eyebrows. "Listen and learn."

"We'd better go," Kelly said. "We only have an hour longer to shop before we're back on Mom duty," she explained to Fisk. "You okay with everything?"

"I'm okay," Fisk reassured them.

They walked off, talking rapidly about how Jodi had kept her knowledge about Lauren a secret. Kelly didn't seem to appreciate it.

It made sense to Fisk, though. Jodi hadn't told them about her past because it didn't matter. Lauren was Lauren. He'd meant what he'd said: she was a good person through and through.

He stood a minute, breathing in the cold air and looking around at the heavily decorated main street of Holiday Point. Now the wreaths on the lampposts didn't bother him. They seemed just right. He waved at a couple of people he knew, and they waved back, not looking surprised that he was sober, not turning away.

He was rebuilding his reputation, even despite the fiasco with his dad.

Speaking of that, though…he'd noticed his phone buzzing a couple of times during the confrontation with the reporter. He pulled it out and saw several messages.

They weren't related to his dad, though; they were from Mrs. Wittinger. Rather than listen to them, he'd fulfill what she actually wanted and deliver her cabinet. He headed toward where Gramps and Lauren stood talking.

Gramps saw him coming and beckoned him to them. "I came as soon as I heard," he said. "No city reporter is gonna bother my granddaughter on my watch." He was breathing hard.

"And I appreciate it, Gramps," Lauren said, "but the drama is over. You can go home."

Fisk shook the man's hand and noticed an odd pallor to his face. "How are you feeling?" he asked Gramps.

"I'm fine, just fine." A frown line creased his forehead.

"Sit down a minute." Fisk gestured toward the open door of Gramps's car. Something about the older man was off. As they walked together toward the car, Gramps stumbled a little. Once he'd sat down sideways on the driver's seat, facing them, Fisk took his pulse.

Lauren had stopped to talk to someone. "What's wrong?" she asked now, approaching them.

Fisk made a snap decision. "I'd like to get your grandfather to the ER."

"What? I'm fine." Gramps waved a hand. "Just a little tired."

Fisk knew he was being overcautious and probably pushy. After all, he was just an army medic, and his training had been a few years back.

Still, he'd always been good at diagnosing patients. And

he'd learned the hard way that everything could go down-hill fast. Better safe than sorry with a man of Gramps's age. "How long have you been feeling tired?"

Lauren jumped in. "He's been complaining about it for the past week."

"I'm just old," Gramps said. "I'll take a nap. I'm fine."

"No, Gramps." Lauren knelt in front of her grandfather, looking worried. "If Fisk thinks you need to go to the ER, you should go."

"Don't you two have something to do? A delivery to make?"

"Forget that," Fisk said. "Your health is more important. Let's go in my truck."

There was a little more haggling, but in the end, Gramps agreed to go. Jodi was enlisted to take care of Bonita, who went with her happily after being reminded she could play with Jodi's kids and her little dog, Mork.

Fisk drove as fast as was safe on the mountain roads, keeping an eye on the man in the seat beside him.

Gramps's hand, on the door grip, was white-knuckled. Lauren sat in the back, leaning forward.

Twenty minutes later, they were at the local emergency room and Gramps was being wheeled in. At that point, Fisk left it to Lauren and the doctors. He yawned and leaned back in his chair. He'd been up late putting the finishing touches on—

Mrs. Wittinger's order.

He checked the time. No way were they going to meet her deadline. She'd be furious. Nothing he could do about it now, though. Gramps Tucker had needed help.

Fisk hoped he hadn't overreacted, scared everyone for no reason. But it was better to be safe.

A little while later, Lauren came into the waiting room

and beckoned to Fisk. "Can you come listen to what the doctor has to say?"

So he did. The doctor, a man Fisk had met a time or two before, shook Fisk's hand. "He needs to be admitted and may need a heart procedure. Good you brought him now."

Good. Each time he helped someone, he earned a little more forgiveness for what had happened with Di and Scarlett.

Fisk listened to what the doctor said and made sure he understood the basics. After the doctor left, and Gramps was dozing, waiting for more tests, Fisk got up to leave.

Lauren was staying, and she wrapped her arms around him. "Thank you so, so much for doing this," she said.

"Shh." He did the hardest thing and unhooked her arms from around him. "It's what anyone would have done."

Her eyes when she looked up at him were wide and speaking.

The fragrance of her hair, orange-blossom-like, tickled his nose.

Her closeness was breaking his heart.

He strode out of the ER, only pausing to click into Mrs. Wittinger's latest voice message, sobbing at him for making her miss an important deadline with her gift.

Fisk would have loved to go home, but he felt bad for letting a customer down. *Just do the next right thing*, he thought, and headed for Mrs. Wittinger's place in his truck.

The day after Gramps had been hospitalized, Lauren prepared for church with her mind already racing.

It had been hard to leave Gramps last night, and Lauren was eager to get back to see him at lunchtime today. At the same time, she'd been eager to get home to Bonita last night. She was going to have to leave her with Jodi again today, so that she could visit Gramps.

She felt impossibly torn between the two of them.

Gramps was doing well, but due to a previous heart condition, he was to stay in the hospital for more tests. A surgical procedure on Tuesday was the goal, if everything checked out. The surgeon was willing to do it on Christmas Eve, and that was what Gramps wanted, too. So they were going through with it.

Having Gramps ill and in the hospital made Lauren's stomach queasy with worry. It also made her realize how much she depended on her grandfather on a daily basis. She tried not to over-rely on him as a caregiver, but the fact was, he was available and eager to care for his great-granddaughter any time Lauren needed for him to do so. They adored each other, which made leaving them together easy and the right thing to do.

She took Bonita into church with her, since it was the children's pageant. Bonita hadn't slept well and now, sleepy, she cuddled against Lauren's chest and watched the pageant and dozed.

That left Lauren's racing mind the opportunity to think about Fisk. He'd sacrificed delivering an order to an influential customer on time on a hunch that an older neighbor needed his help. What man she'd known before had even had those kinds of hunches?

Fisk was a big tough guy, but he was also caring and emotionally aware. It was a potent combination, and she was losing her ability to resist it.

But Fisk had let her know, and reminded her again yesterday, that he wasn't up for a relationship. Thinking of how she'd thrown her arms around him—twice—and had him gently remove her from him—twice, also—made her face heat.

After church, she heard Mrs. Wittinger lamenting the fact that Fisk hadn't delivered her project on time. When Lauren had tried to explain why Fisk was late, the older woman had waved a hand, silencing her. "Please," she'd said, "I don't need explanations. I can perfectly well imagine what caused the delay." She'd looked Lauren up and down as if she were somehow scandalous, in a convincing enough way that Lauren looked down to remind herself that, yes, she was wearing casual black pants and a puffy black-and-white top with a high neck. Nothing to see here, that was for sure.

After Mrs. Wittinger had moved on, her housekeeper approached, an apologetic expression on her face. "I wanted you to know that Fisk did deliver that piece of furniture," she said. "It was late, but everything worked out fine. I don't know what she's complaining about."

As exhausted as he was, Fisk had delivered the cabinet? By himself? And he was still being cut down about his work ethic?

That just wasn't fair.

Leaving Bonita with Jodi for the second day in a row was tough. Lauren knew she was safe with Jodi, but the way Bonita had cried when Lauren left was still tearing at her heart as she trudged into the hospital. Jodi had texted her that this was a normal development, separation anxiety starting up. Good to know, but that didn't make Bonita's wails completely stop echoing in Lauren's mind.

She entered Gramps's room. He lay in the bed, mouth a little open as he slept, and a surge of love for him washed over her. He was family, her and Bonita's closest family, and she intended to take care of him. She moved his half-eaten food tray and straightened his bedcovers.

He woke up and they talked through how he was feeling, how his night had gone, what the doctors said was in store for him today.

And then he waved a hand, his IV flapping. "Enough about my health. Upshot is, I'm gonna be fine. Now tell me what's bothering you."

Let me count the things. She didn't want him to worry about Bonita's new separation anxiety, so she told him how Mrs. Wittinger was criticizing Fisk, even though he'd ended up delivering her item on the day he'd been scheduled to do it, if a little bit later in the day.

"And that hurts you because you care for him," Gramps said in his blunt way.

Lauren opened her mouth to protest and then closed it again. Gramps was the wisest person she knew. There was no fooling him. "Yeah," she said. "Yeah. I do care for him. A lot."

"I think the feeling is returned," Gramps said.

Lauren couldn't help smiling at the thought, but she quickly sobered. "That may be, but he won't be with me. Says he can't."

"Why's that?" Gramps pushed the lever on his hospital bed, raising the back higher. Someone in blue-green scrubs came in and cleared away the remains of Gramps's lunch, then entered some information on an electronic tablet she carried with her.

After the woman left, Gramps refocused immediately. "Why does Fisk think he can't be with you?"

"He feels like he did something wrong in Baltimore. I can't share the details, but it was pretty bad. Still, I'm not sure he's as at fault as he thinks he is."

Gramps looked thoughtful. "He's a veteran. Wartime experiences can make you feel guilty. It can bleed over into your civilian life." He sipped from a cup with a bent straw. "Point is, you may have to nudge him. Help him see that he's worthy of having a happy life."

Lauren leaned back in the hard plastic chair and looked out the window at the bare trees beyond. "I don't know how to do that. Talking doesn't work."

"Wouldn't, with a man like Fisk."

"I wish I could find out what really happened in Baltimore, that night when Fisk…that night in question," she self-corrected. Fisk's story was his own to tell. "I feel like there's a piece of the puzzle missing."

"You do have a cousin in Baltimore," Gramps reminded her.

"Of course. Carrie." Up until now, Lauren hadn't connected the two parts of her life, a family member who lived in the same community where Fisk's disastrous accident had happened. "I wonder if she'd know anything about it."

"She does research and marketing for one of the towns on the outskirts of Baltimore," Gramps said. "You could ask her what she could find out. Real bright girl. In fact, hasn't she been begging you to visit?"

"She has," Lauren said. "We haven't seen each other for years, but we reconnected on social media recently."

In fact, Carrie had reached out to Lauren after seeing the headlines about her ex-husband. But unlike some old friends, Carrie hadn't been looking for information to fuel the raging fire of gossip. She'd been kind, concerned about how Lauren was handling it.

"If you visited her," Gramps said, "you could bring Bonita. Her baby's about the same age. Maybe you could find out a little more about what happened."

Lauren listened to the beeping of a monitor down the hall. Someone was mopping outside the door, and the smell of disinfectant wafted in.

The idea of taking action to help Fisk appealed to her—a lot—but it also seemed like a long shot. What were the chances that Carrie would know something?

On the other hand, Carrie *was* a local and a researcher, and smart as a whip.

Visiting her cousin would be a treat. More than that, it would be a chance to maybe help someone she really cared about.

Her work as Fisk's office manager was mostly done. With Christmas falling in the middle of the week this year, most people would focus the next few days on home and family. There was time for a quick trip to Baltimore.

But there was one huge obstacle to the plan. She shook her head at Gramps. "I can't leave you here, alone."

"I'm anything but alone." Gramps held up his cell phone, where notifications from calls and messages filled the screen. "There are way too many people who want to visit me, for you to stay around all the time. They only allow two visitors at a time, so…"

"So I'm taking up too much of your space and time?" She laughed.

"I didn't want to rush you, but I think there's a crowd in the waiting room."

She stood, leaned down and kissed Gramps. "Thank you," she said. "You're a genius. But call me if there's anything at all that you need, and I'll tell the nurses the same thing."

"Get outta here," he said, waving her away. "See you Tuesday in the recovery room."

As she left the hospital, her spirits lifted. She'd check

with Carrie, and do some online research tonight to figure out an approach.

She wouldn't have much time, but that just meant she'd be motivated. She had to find out what had really happened on the day Fisk had lost his girlfriend and daughter. She simply couldn't believe Fisk was at fault in the way he believed he was. Fisk was a good man, good to the core. The trouble was, he didn't trust himself.

Maybe it would be a wild-goose chase. Probably so, in fact. But it was the only thing she could think of to do, the only way she could help this man she was coming to care for so much. She had to make the effort, for Fisk's sake.

She wanted him to have the same freedom she felt herself. She'd been imprisoned by fear of tabloid reporters who could ruin her life and Bonita's. But then she'd found this place where people still paid attention to your character, not just your online profile. Where people supported others who were changing and growing.

For Fisk to embrace all the good that Holiday Point could give him, he at least needed to explore the past. Maybe she could make it happen.

Minutes after she sent the text to Carrie, she got an excited, emoji-filled text in return.

It looked like she and Bonita were going for an overnight road trip.

Chapter Thirteen

It took a while for Fisk to realize that Lauren was gone.

He thought nothing of her being absent the first couple of hours of work. She had her grandfather to consider. In fact, he'd almost texted her to tell her he'd watch Bonita while she visited the hospital, but he'd hesitated, and she hadn't asked. She must have gotten Jodi to watch the baby again.

When she didn't call and didn't communicate by noon, he was...*off*. He was used to having her around. And sure, they weren't that busy now; it was Christmas week, and thanks to her, they were pretty much caught up. Most people were deep into their holiday preparations and wouldn't be placing new orders this week. He would deliver the last couple of items later today, and then he'd be done.

Nemo kept looking toward the door, and once, he jumped his paws up to the windowsill to look in the direction of Gramps and Lauren's house.

Late afternoon, Fisk couldn't stand it anymore. He left Nemo at home and went to the hospital, where he learned that Gramps was doing well but couldn't accept any more visitors today. Jodi was turned away at the same time, so he asked how she was doing caring for Bonita.

"I'm not," she'd said. "Well, I did yesterday, and it was great, but I haven't seen her or Lauren today."

He checked with an orderly he knew and learned that Lauren hadn't been in to visit Gramps today, either.

What?

Was she…gone?

It was hard to fathom that she'd leave her grandfather alone on the eve of surgery.

She would leave Fisk, for sure. That would be right of her. He'd made it clear they had no chance of a relationship.

Still, for her to ditch a job without notice was unlike her.

He also didn't think she was the kind of person who'd leave a friend or relative without any kind of reason why.

Maybe something had happened to her. He texted Gramps and his brothers and a few other friends, asking if they knew where Lauren was.

There was some worried chatter on the group text, and then Gramps silenced it. Lauren was okay, he said. She and Bonita had headed out of town to visit a relative. She was safe and enjoying herself.

As Fisk walked out of the hospital, he checked his text messages again and there was one from Lauren. She apologized for forgetting to let him know she needed a little time off.

He made his final deliveries and then found himself driving around in his truck. He didn't want to go home.

Nothing had happened to Lauren, which was a huge relief. But she'd left him in the lurch. He couldn't depend on her.

Not that he should. He had no right to expect it. They had no real commitment to each other, even professionally.

How had she infiltrated his life and his heart so quickly?

In the face of this kind of emptiness, Fisk knew only two possible places to go. Into a bottle, as he'd done in the past. Or to the Lord.

He'd missed church yesterday, and he figured the sanctuary would be locked. The church office was closed on Mondays, and this week, everyone would be resting up for the big push of Christmas Eve and Day.

There was one place, though, where the church was always open, and where spiritual wisdom abounded. He turned down the road toward his grandmother's nursing home.

He was in the chapel, praying, when someone gripped his shoulder.

"What are you doing in here when you don't have to be?"

It was his grandmother.

"Just looking for a church." He stood and kissed her downy cheek. "I know I can pray anywhere, but sometimes having the right environment helps. Plus I get to see you. Get your take on some things."

"Happy to listen." She leaned her head against him for just a second. Then she straightened. "When you're done talking to the Man upstairs, come to my room."

"I will." He hugged her.

After she left, he did what he knew he should do as a Christian: he prayed for forgiveness. For all the wrongs he'd done, but especially, for Scarlett and Di.

He'd done it before, many times. He knew intellectually that he was forgiven; could cite verses about it. The Bible said that if he forgave others, and confessed his own sins, he'd be forgiven. Forgiveness of sins was what Christ had died for.

So why couldn't he feel it?

He'd worked hard, so hard. With God's help, he'd pulled himself up out of alcoholism. He'd started a business, partly as a way to redeem himself in the community, and with Lauren's help he'd fulfilled all of his Christmas orders.

But hard work wouldn't lead to happiness and fulfill-ment, not by itself. He still felt empty. Still felt like a bad person.

Lauren had left. Well, he was upset, but not surprised. It was retribution for what he'd done. Or rather, what he'd not done.

Now he had to make the best of the part of his life he had left. Not only did he have to contribute to society, help and serve others, but he also needed to be content while doing it. God had made him and walked beside him. That had to be enough.

His discontent, he figured, was an insult to God. So he prayed for forgiveness for that, too.

When he stood up, he felt marginally better.

He headed toward his grandmother's room, planning on a quick chat. He needed to get home, and 8 p.m. was late for her.

"Fisk! In here!" A voice tugged him toward a large lounge area, where at least ten women were gathered. Some stood around a table of food, while others sat doing some kind of craft.

Gramma was in the craft group. He sat down beside her and put an arm lightly around her shoulders. He squinted at the red, white and green yarn in front of her. "What are you working on?"

"My book club—that's these ladies—we're in charge of the decorations at Christmas dinner. And we're behind schedule." She held up a knitted flower. "We're supposed to make these for every person attending, but I don't think we'll get there."

"We could make something quicker," one of the other ladies suggested.

"Like a bookmark." That idea came from Penny Hamlin, librarian of the residential facility.

"That's simple," Fisk said. "Even I could do that."

His grandmother raised her eyebrows, then dug in her bag and held out a couple of knitting needles. "Do you need me to cast on for you?"

He hadn't expected her to take him seriously. "Uh... sure. Yes, please."

Fisk knew how to knit, or at least, he remembered it after watching Penny for a couple of minutes. Another soldier had taught him when they'd faced long stretches of boredom in the Middle East. When Gramma handed him the needles with a short row of stitches cast on, his hands found the rhythm quickly.

While they knitted, Fisk asked questions, and the women talked comfortably. The book club met every month, sometimes more often. They were the "fun" book club; there was another one whose members prided themselves on heavy religious and philosophical texts, but Gramma's club always chose popular fiction, mysteries being their current favorite. "Plus, we have better food," Penny explained. "You should get a plate and take some home. We have at least four different cakes."

"I'd definitely choose this club," Fisk assured them.

"You've sure changed," said one of the other women who was dressed in athletic clothes. "You used to come in here drunk as a skunk."

Fisk winced. "I apologize for that. To all of you."

"Well, you were funny," Gramma said. "But I like you better sober."

The others nodded agreement. "And you're a lot more productive at crafting than you used to be." Penny pointed at Fisk's bookmark, which had grown by a couple of inches already while they'd been talking.

Fisk marveled at the women's easy forgiveness of his former obnoxiousness, and their acceptance that he was a changed man. It felt like fresh, cold water flowing over him.

They'd forgiven him. *God* had forgiven him. Could he finally forgive himself?

He handed his bookmark off to his grandmother to finish. "Can I pick you up and bring you to the Wilkins Christmas Eve tomorrow?"

She raised her eyebrows. "At your mom and dad's? No, thank you."

"We talked them into doing an early version of their party," Fisk explained. "The afternoon will be family-friendly. We can leave before it gets wild later."

"We'd still have time to go to church Christmas Eve?"

"Yes. That's part of why we talked them into the change."

"Then I'll go, and thank you," Gramma said, and they made arrangements for a pickup time and place.

Just a few days ago, he'd actually invited Lauren to the party. That had been part of his thinking in advocating for the early version of the party, too. Family-friendly meant Lauren-friendly. He didn't want to expose her to anything ugly.

Now that connection with her seemed to have dissolved.

They hadn't known each other long, after all. They'd shared one kiss. There were no expectations between them, or there shouldn't have been.

Only now that the thing between them was gone did he realize that he *had* been developing expectations, or at least hopes. Their collapse left a hole in him that ached sometimes and throbbed sometimes, but was always there. *Take it away, Lord, if it's Your will.*

If the Lord didn't take it away, then Fisk would just have to learn to bear the emptiness. Or…could he push for Lauren somehow, fight for her?

Lauren returned to Holiday Point midday on the twenty-fourth, with a brand-new friend in tow. Two of them, actually. Cerise Johnson was the type who'd never met a stranger, and her three-year-old daughter seemed to have inherited the social gene. The daughter and Bonita had laughed and played during the entire car ride from Baltimore to Holiday Point.

Lauren's cousin had started researching immediately after hearing from Lauren. Carrie had unearthed Cerise's story and contacted her, and Cerise had been happy to meet with them, especially when Lauren had told her Fisk's version of that awful day's events.

She was even happy to make the trip up from Baltimore with Lauren. She was willing, even eager, to share her slightly different version of the tragic day with Fisk. Plus, she had family in Uniontown and welcomed the ride to visit them.

And so here they were, pulling up to the Wilkins family party at Fisk's parents' house.

In the end, Lauren couldn't just drop Cerise off at the Wilkins party and pick her up in an hour, as she'd planned. Not when she saw the crowd. Cam's family and Alec's, a few people she'd met at the diner, Fisk's grandma and his parents. There were lots of kids and several dogs. And of course, Fisk himself. He was circulating, talking to everyone.

With all those people, there was a real possibility that Cerise, who used a cane due to leg issues stemming from the shooting, would be knocked right off her feet. Plus the party was being held outside, in the unseasonably warm December air, with a bonfire burning. Nice, but there was a lot of mud and uneven ground that could trip Cerise up.

The real truth was, Lauren couldn't resist staying in Fisk's vicinity, once she'd seen him. She wanted to know what happened when Cerise told her story.

So she got Bonita out of her car seat and walked with her toward the party, just behind Cerise and her toddler.

In addition to their research in Baltimore, she and Carrie had gone shopping. Bonita had a new Christmas outfit, red-and-white striped tights and a frilly red dress with a white lace collar.

She looked adorable. People stopped them to say so, and Bonita flung her arm out and twirled and smiled, basking in the attention. She was no shrinking violet, and Lauren was glad. Bonita was going to do something big someday.

Lindsay, the teenager who'd taken care of Bonita before, was here, apparently because she was friends with a Wilkins cousin. She swooped Bonita up and insisted on carrying her around, to Bonita's delight.

Fisk, Cam and Alec stood around their parents, basically encircling them, talking seriously. When they all finally laughed, Lauren felt a boost inside. Maybe they were starting to work it out. That would be so, so good for Fisk.

There was another brother, Frank, who never came home due to all the family issues. Maybe the family could repair itself enough to heal that rift.

When the conversation among the brothers and their parents broke up, Lauren took a few sideways steps to where she was in Fisk's line of sight.

He looked at her and visibly jolted. Was he *that* surprised to see her? He'd mentioned this party to her a few days ago and though he'd said she probably wouldn't enjoy it, the invitation had seemed to be open still.

Cerise was off chatting with someone—that "never met a stranger" thing—so Lauren faced Fisk alone, watching as he spoke to someone and then marched over.

"I thought you were gone," he said.

She shook her head. "I told you I might take some days off when the rush was over." She said it guiltily because she knew she'd told him when he wasn't paying attention.

Right before leaving, she'd thought she should at least call him, but she hadn't wanted to get into a big, involved discussion about why she might be leaving. She was afraid she'd reveal too much. So she'd just sent a vague text and taken off.

Which was unprofessional and rude. "I'm sorry. I should have discussed it with you before I took off."

"Yeah."

"It was for a good reason, believe me."

Fisk studied her, looked away, and then looked back. "You're under my skin. I feel it when you leave."

Not what she'd expected him to say. She could barely look away from his intense eyes and then she had to, because she felt way too breathless. "I'm actually here for a reason," she said. "I'd like for you to meet someone."

Chapter Fourteen

Fisk followed Lauren past small clusters of laughing, chatting guests, feeling very off-kilter.

Lauren had left. He'd resigned himself to that.

Now here she was, acting like nothing was wrong, bringing him to meet someone at his own family's party. It didn't compute.

She reached back and took his hand. Took his hand! When he'd thought he'd never feel her soft skin or see that long shiny hair or hear her voice again.

He was a little mad and a lot relieved. She was still in his life.

She tugged him toward an area where several moms were letting their kids play in an icy drift of snow that hadn't yet melted. "Hey, Cerise?" she said to a woman younger than Fisk.

The woman stood with the help of a cane. "Come here, honey," she said to a toddler, and the little girl came.

Fisk got the same kind of jolt he often did when he met a baby or young child: Would Scarlett have been like this? The feeling washed over him like an ocean wave, nearly knocking him over and then drifting back to wherever it had come from.

He guessed he'd have that his whole life.

Lauren introduced him to the woman, whose name was Cerise Johnson.

The woman shook his hand. "There's no easy way to say this. I was there the night you lost your wife and baby."

Di wasn't my wife. The stray thought shielded him for just a few seconds, and then the other, bigger, more painful revelation hit him. "You were there?"

"Yes. That's how I got injured." She gestured toward her leg and her cane. "But this one wasn't hurt." She nodded toward the little girl, who'd plopped down and was squeezing handfuls of snow and rocks and dirt between her fingers, laughing.

Fisk swallowed. "I'm glad she wasn't hurt," he said through a tight throat.

"She says," Cerise nodded toward Lauren, "she says when you were running after the bad guys, you heard your baby crying."

Fisk felt sucker punched. He couldn't look at Lauren. She'd shared that with a stranger?

"I'm sorry," Lauren said, touching his arm briefly, "but this is important. Think back. Did you hear a lot of babies crying, or just one?"

Was she torturing him on purpose? "Just one." The sound of that lone wail had echoed in his dreams ever since.

"Honey," Cerise said, "that was my baby crying. Not yours."

Her words confused him. "No, that was Scarlett."

She put a hand on his arm and looked at him with a steady, brown-eyed gaze. "It wasn't," she said simply. "I was there. I saw the whole thing, and…your baby was gone. Instantly, I'd suspect. There was no other little one crying except mine."

Lauren made a little sound, like she was holding back tears herself.

"Wait." Fisk was trying to understand. Could what Cerise said be true?

He sucked in a breath as his view of what had happened that night rearranged itself.

If Scarlett hadn't been crying, then… "You're saying Scarlett was…gone, instantly?"

The woman nodded, her face twisting in sympathy. Lauren was biting her lip.

Fisk didn't know how to feel.

Should he be glad he hadn't run away when his child was crying for him, or sad that she'd had a few less moments of life on this earth?

"You helped bring those men down," Cerise said. "They've been a plague in our community for years. I'm grateful to you."

He nodded and tried to smile.

She must have seen that he needed time to process all of this, that his throat was getting too tight to speak. "One other thing. Lauren said you'd told her you were drinking that day. But you seemed stone-cold sober to me."

"I…had a beer. Hours earlier." No point in trying to pull anything over on this woman. Nor on Lauren. He couldn't even remember why, exactly, he'd told her he was drinking.

Cerise gave him a quick hug. "I sure am sorry for what happened to your family."

Fisk swallowed hard and croaked out a thank-you, feeling like his insides had been scraped raw.

She looked over at Lauren. "If it's okay with you, I need to go," she said. She turned to Fisk and explained. "My folks live in Uniontown and we're having our own party tonight."

"You're driving her?" he asked Lauren.

Lauren nodded.

Around them, people were still talking and laughing. Kids ran off their excess energy. The sun was sinking lower, the air getting colder.

Cerise fumbled in a diaper bag, pulled out a packet of baby wipes and knelt to clean her muddy toddler's hands.

Fisk was trying to understand what had just happened. He looked at Lauren and then at Cerise. "But how did you…" He broke off, too overwhelmed to finish the question.

"She found me, man," Cerise said, nodding toward Lauren. "She came to Baltimore and found me. You've got a smart, persistent friend here. She has your good at heart."

Lauren had made this happen? Had gone to Baltimore and found this woman?

He wanted to talk to her, find out all about it. Really, he wanted to sit with her, maybe hold her, while he thought through what Cerise had told him. Just having her there would mean everything.

But she was busy thanking Lindsay, the teenager who'd babysat for her before, and who'd apparently been holding Bonita.

"Ready when you are," Cerise said to Lauren, taking her own child by the hand.

"Let's go." Lauren scooped up Bonita, gave Fisk a small wave and led Cerise toward the car area.

He got the distinct feeling that her wave meant "I've done all I can do. It's in your hands now."

That night was Christmas Eve, and Lauren was so exhausted that she considered not going to church. She'd driven to Baltimore and back, and then driven Cerise to

Uniontown, all of it with Bonita in tow. Bonita was a good traveler, but she'd finally gotten fussy on the way back from Uniontown, and no wonder. Her nap schedule had been disrupted and she'd been in too many new environments with new people.

Lauren had gone to visit Gramps, of course, as soon as she'd returned, foisting Bonita off on Kelly for a couple of hours, steeling herself to her baby's cries and talking back to her mom-guilt. She had to see her grandfather, too.

Gramps had come through his procedure fine and was awake enough to hear the basics of Lauren's visit to her cousin. When he'd gotten tired, she had gone to Kelly's to pick up Bonita, taken her home and fed her dinner.

Lauren wanted nothing more than to go to bed, but it was Christmas Eve. She needed the spiritual uplift of celebrating Christ's birth with her new church family.

Needed to focus on faith, not on what might or might not be going on with Fisk.

She was glad she'd gone to Baltimore and, with her cousin's help, located Cerise. Fisk needed to know he hadn't left his baby in need, that there had been no way he could have saved her. At the same time, that knowledge had to have brought up all the pain Fisk felt around the accident. She hoped he was okay, but she'd done all she could. Hopefully, he could start to move on.

She pulled into the church parking lot and got out of the car, shivering. Temperatures had dropped and there was a light snow falling. It was an hour until services started—she'd gotten the time wrong—but that was fine. Lauren walked with Bonita toward the nursery. She'd offer to help there while participants in the live nativity were getting organized and the congregation started to drift in.

As soon as she got inside the church, she was surrounded by concerned people who wanted to know how Gramps was doing. She explained, over and over, that he'd come through his procedure well and that the doctor on duty expected to release him tomorrow, so that he could spend Christmas night, at least, at home.

She and Bonita had almost reached the nursery when Jodi rushed up. "We need you and the baby outside. Now."

"What?" Lauren picked up Bonita.

"We need you in the live nativity. You have to be Mary, and Bonita needs to be the baby Jesus."

"But—"

"Didn't you get my text? The current Mary's sister is sick, and she had to go to Delaware. I told you this might happen."

"I didn't see a text. It must have failed to send, maybe?"

"Oh, I'm sorry." Jodi's brows drew together. "That's my fault, I should have called you, too. But you'll do it, won't you? We need to get you dressed, like, now."

"Dressed in what?" But she was already following Jodi to the women's room, where a toga-type garment for her and a swaddling blanket for Bonita were waiting.

She put the toga on and wrapped Bonita. Jodi produced a head covering and attached it. "See? Perfect. You're about the same size."

"Wait, don't tell, me," Lauren said darkly. "Fisk's playing Joseph."

"No, he's not. It's Cam, actually. You'll be fine."

Relieved and yet somehow disappointed, Lauren followed Jodi outside to where the other members of the cast were setting up in a makeshift shed, fortunately warmed with a space heater.

"Thanks for stepping in," Cam said from under his Joseph costume. "All we do is take care of the baby. No lines or anything."

Lauren nodded down at Bonita, who was sitting up in the manger, waving and babbling. "Still, we may have our hands full."

The other cast members assembled around them.

"Nee! Nee!" Bonita shouted, pointing.

And there was Nemo, looking ridiculous in a white and pink sheep costume.

Where Nemo was, Fisk couldn't be far away. She studied the other actors more closely. One of the shepherds was taller and broader-shouldered than the other two.

Fisk.

He was helping a lanky teenager move a bale of hay, joking and laughing with the boy.

And then they were told to take their places, and people started coming by on their way into services, oohing and aahing, laughing when Bonita posed and smiled and broke into baby-chatter.

Fisk and the other shepherds walked together toward the manger. The three kings came from the other direction. One of them she recognized as Tonya, who wore a penciled-in mustache and heavy eyebrows that made her look more like a pirate than a Biblical-era king.

"How's Gramps Tucker?" Cam asked across the manger during a break in the spectators.

"He's doing well," she said quietly. "He may get to come home tomorrow, just in time to watch Bonita open her presents."

"That's great." Cam smiled at her. "Great what you did for Fisk earlier today, too. I don't know exactly what happened, but he looks like a big load has been shifted off his back."

They both looked at Fisk, who was laughing with the other shepherds, head thrown back, eyes crinkling.

"I'm glad he's feeling better," she said quietly.

As their audience grew, Lauren settled back into her Mary role. She rubbed Bonita's back until she lay down, and thanked God that Fisk seemed better. That they'd had safe travels and that she'd renewed ties with her cousin. That Gramps had come through his procedure well and should be home tomorrow.

More people were filing by now, and Lauren and Bonita were once again the center of attention. It was what she'd hoped to avoid in Holiday Point, and yet, she didn't mind. She trusted the members of this community to treat her with kindness, not judgment.

Moreover, she trusted God to lead her in the right direction and protect her from harm. If another reporter came and spread dirt about her, she'd handle it with the help of God, her little family and her faith community.

Nemo let out a sharp bark, making everyone laugh. But he'd been alerting them to something real: a squirrel was running by, and Kelly's dog, a retired racing greyhound in a reindeer costume, took off after it.

"Pokey!" Kelly, who'd been in the earlier part of the show as pregnant Mary, rushed after the dog. Alec, one of the kings, and Cam both jumped up to help her while Fisk calmed Nemo and the other animal portraying a sheep, a blind-and-deaf schnauzer who seemed to know something was going on and wanted to join in. Lauren watched, patting Bonita's back. Lauren's job right now was to be a mother, just like Mary's job had been to mother Jesus for a time. In the midst of the chaos in the little shelter, she felt peace.

Finally, Pokey was caught and scolded, and everyone returned to their stations. The spectators were cheering and laughing and talking, any ice between them broken—the Christmas Eve service was one where community members without a church home often attended, and it was good to see the regular congregation connecting with them.

Lauren glanced up and saw that Fisk's eyes were locked on hers. *Thank you*, he mouthed to her.

She smiled a little, even though she wasn't sure what he was thanking her for. Helping with Pokey? Bringing Cerise?

She sucked in a breath and refocused on Bonita, the surroundings, and the Bible readings that were beginning. The live nativity crew processed into the church and sat together, and the meaning of the service and the day swept over Lauren in a different way.

She'd never thought, before, about what it would be like to be Mary. Disgraced in many people's eyes for being pregnant. Traveling without much support, having to find shelter.

And yet, she was now celebrated and revered for her role in bringing the Christ child into the world. All because she'd ignored public opinion and followed God's will.

Public opinion. It had governed Lauren's flight to Holiday Point, and had worried her throughout her time here, but it was meaningless.

Her heart tender and her throat tight, she listened to the preaching and took part in the singing and praying. She inhaled the scent of pine boughs and candles and admired the Christmas decorations all around the church. Looked at the people, many of whom were becoming friends in such a short time.

Was Fisk a friend? Would she even see him again?

It was out of her control. But because she didn't want to test herself too much, she slipped out of church after the service was over and headed home alone.

Chapter Fifteen

On Christmas morning, just as the sun peeked golden out of the snow-covered trees, Fisk walked from his place to Lauren's.

His arms were full, as befit a Christmas Day visit. He slipped and slid on the icy footpath, Nemo trotting nimbly beside him.

His heart was full, too, to overflowing. After yesterday, after last night, he'd gone home and slept like a child and awakened with this new joy in his heart. It had to do with taking another leap forward in his faith. *Broken is open* was an AA saying. His own brokenness had removed his resistance to fully relying on God. Too, the emotional events of yesterday had broken a dam inside of him, and the result was a tidal wave of feeling for Lauren. Feelings so deep he was tripping on them.

He approached the front door of Gramps's cottage like a sweaty-handed kid on his first date. And then he saw her through the window, and his heart just about stopped.

She sat in a rocking chair beside the fire, her expression pensive. The mantel was decorated with ribbons and greenery. Bonita lay against her chest, head on her mother's shoulder, asleep. After last night, the comparison with Mary and Jesus was obvious.

She glanced up and caught his eye, and it wasn't Mary at all; it was Lauren in all her beautiful, imperfect perfection. She smiled, but almost immediately, a shadow of doubt and resistance crossed her face.

That was something they'd have to overcome if they were to have a chance. Was there even a "they," anyway?

Don't rush things, he counseled himself.

Fisk hadn't planned for his thoughts to take this direction, but they had. Those unformed, mushy feelings of love were arranging themselves into a structure. A family structure. With him and Lauren at the center of it.

Could it happen? He didn't know, but he saw with clarity as bright as the snow glistening in the new light that he wanted it.

He approached the door, and it opened as he and Nemo arrived. Lauren was there with the baby still asleep on her shoulder, holding a finger to her lips.

Nemo barked.

"Quiet." Fisk put a hand on the dog's head.

The baby shifted a little, then relaxed. They went inside, and Fisk slipped off his boots and wiped Nemo's feet.

Inside, the whole place smelled like cinnamon rolls. Just like one long-ago time when he'd slept over at the house of a friend with a roundish, hugging type of mother. That was the smell he'd awakened to in the morning, and he'd known it was what he wanted for himself. He'd forgotten about it, but now he remembered vividly.

"Is your grandfather home? How's he doing?"

"Later today." She closed the door behind him. She was moving gingerly, clearly trying not to rouse Bonita. "He got through the night well."

"That's good." Fisk had grown to think of Gramps Tucker as a relative. He'd been a source of fatherly wisdom to Fisk since Fisk had moved here. "I tried to see him, but he had too many visitors."

She smiled. "Tell me about it. Take off your coat." She gestured toward the row of pegs by the door.

She didn't seem put out by his visit, but he still felt awkward because he'd come over without an invitation. He held up the two wrapped packages he'd brought. "I wanted to give you and Bonita your gifts."

Her hand flew to her mouth. "I didn't get you anything."

"You got me everything. You got me Cerise."

She smiled, the sunshine breaking out after clouds. "Good. You see it as the gift it was meant to be. Come sit by the fire."

There were two chairs there, and he took the one Gramps Tucker usually sat in. Nemo sat in front of the fire, staring at Bonita, then yipping.

"Nemo!" Fisk snapped his fingers. "Quiet!"

"He wants her to wake up. It's fine." Lauren laughed.

Bonita lifted her head and looked around, blinking.

Lauren set Bonita down on the hearthrug beside Nemo, then checked that the fireplace screen was secure.

Fisk wanted to be clear about how he felt, how grateful he was. "I mean it about Cerise being a gift. I know I'm forgiven by God, and I know I couldn't have saved Scarlett ultimately, but it was killing me to think that she was scared and in pain at the end, and I wasn't there to comfort her."

"Worst nightmare." Lauren shook her head, her forehead creasing.

He didn't want this visit to be all about him and his history, his inner issues. "Is this your first holiday without your husband?"

"Second," she said.

He did the math. "Were you pregnant when he…got arrested?"

She nodded. "Pretty far along. That was part of the tabloid appeal. Lots of moral indignation for a star who's cheating on his pregnant wife. With underage girls." Her tone was bland, but there was a depth of pain in her eyes.

He'd never looked up the news articles about Lauren's ex. It would have felt like an invasion of her privacy. But it must have been terribly traumatic for her. "Do you think you'll ever get over it?" he asked. And then he realized that he was asking for two reasons: out of concern for her as a friend, but also out of wanting to know whether she felt like she could be in a relationship.

"Not over it," she said slowly. "But more able to put it aside and move on." She bit her lip. "I blamed myself for not seeing the signs. And I've doubted myself because I made a bad choice in a husband."

"Love isn't real rational."

"No, it's not. But I think it's going to be okay. I feel my faith really growing through this tough time. I've started reading the Bible more and more, and I want to keep it up. I feel like if I know it better and rely on it, I'll have more confidence in my decisions. Make better ones."

Bonita reached her arms up to him, and Fisk took her. The novelty of having him rock her kept her content for a while, especially when he found her stuffed dog and wiggled it in front of her, making it talk.

Scarlett had liked that. The memory hurt, but it wasn't all he felt. He realized he wanted to know Bonita for herself. What was *she* like? How would she grow?

He and Lauren talked, really talked, while Bonita played in his lap and then on the floor with Nemo and a board book and a plastic truck, and then back into her mom's lap for another nap. They talked about it all: his alcoholism, his trauma from the accident and what he still needed to do to push his healing along. And she talked about watching her father go through two rehabs and turn back to drinking, worse each time. That made her skeptical of people who said they'd recovered from their drinking problem.

Fisk put his hands out like stop signs. "Not me. I haven't recovered. I think I'll always go to at least one AA meeting per week."

"Good. I'm glad you're taking it seriously and being careful."

She brought out cinnamon rolls, and they stuffed themselves, giving Bonita little bites as well. Lauren opened the carved wooden dog Fisk had made for Bonita, and the picture frame he'd made for her. He had framed a photo he'd taken one day when she, Gramps and Bonita had been outside in the snow.

She loved the gifts, it was obvious, and she said so. The way she looked at Fisk told him she got it, what he'd meant by the gifts. For him, making things for her and her baby was a way of wooing her.

When the talking and the eating and the gift opening was done, the sun had risen high enough to put the snow sparkling. And Fisk had one other thing he needed to do. "Speaking of moving my healing along…would you and Bonita like to go for a walk?"

"Sure," she said, "if you'll take turns carrying her. She's getting so heavy."

"I'll do you one better." He unfolded his child-carrier backpack, the one he'd only had Scarlett in a few times. He set it on the floor. "Put her in."

"You're sure?" She was looking at him steadily and he saw that she understood the significance of that, too. That it was Scarlett's, and that using it with Bonita was a way of moving on, but also saying goodbye.

When had she gotten to know him so well?

Finding it a little hard to speak, he just nodded. And she put Bonita into the carrier and helped him strap it on his back. He was pretty sure she noticed the couple of tears he'd swiped away, but she pretended not to.

As they headed out down the sunny, snowy road, Lauren kept stealing glances at Bonita, high on Fisk's back.

Well, in truth, she was looking at Fisk, too. He and the baby were both smiling, obviously enjoying each other and the day. Nemo trotted alongside Fisk, head and tail held high.

A cardinal, fire-engine red, flew across the road and landed on the spidery branch of a tree. Bir-DEE, Bir-DEE, chuh-chuh-chuh-chuh-chuh, it called, and a moment later, the call was answered. The cardinal flew away.

Fisk took her hand, and she let him. They'd just shared a lot of what was inside of each of them. No more secrets, and being close felt right.

Her effort, what she'd come to in prayer this morning, was to open herself to love but keep God at the forefront and center.

"This is nice." He squeezed her mitten-clad hand.

"It is."

"Would you…look, Lauren, I'm bursting to tell you something I probably shouldn't."

Dread clutched at her stomach, but she forced herself to keep walking. "Is it a good something or a bad something?"

"Depends on how you feel about it."

"What is it?" Something in his voice told her it was serious.

She looked over at him. His face seemed carved of wood. Bonita reached down and patted his cheek, offering a sympathetic "ba-ba-ba-ba-ba."

Lauren could barely catch her breath.

Fisk stopped, turned and took both of her hands in his, Nemo cooperatively sitting at a right angle to them, head cocked, eyes alert. "I've fallen in love with you."

She gulped. Met his eyes and then looked away, trying to frown thoughtfully.

Inside, she was doing cartwheels.

But keep God at the center. Was the love he felt of God? Was her own feeling toward him of God?

She'd proceed cautiously. "I… I'm starting to have feelings for you, too."

"Are you?" He let out a huge sigh as if he were relieved, and squeezed her hands. "I admire so much about you. You're a great mom, and granddaughter, and you're a mastermind business person…"

The word *mastermind* made her snort.

"Speaking of that, I hope you'll consider staying on as my office manager."

"Really?" She blinked at the shift, but this felt like safer, less emotional ground. She could deal with that.

"Really," he said. "How else am I going to organize the new slew of orders you've helped me to get?"

She bit her lip, looked at him. Tried not to smile, but the corners of her mouth kept curving up. "I probably can stay on."

He gave her a quick hug and then backed away. "Sorry. I'm excited and nervous."

"Nervous?" She was, too, but she wasn't quite sure why.

"Yes, because there's more. A lot more. I want to start

seeing you, dating, being a couple. Are you…is there any chance you're up for that?"

More inner cartwheels. "I haven't always made the best choices. In relationships. That is…" She stopped and thought about her marriage. "Actually, just the once, but it was a really, really bad choice."

"And you think I'm right in line with your bad choices." He studied her, his forehead wrinkled.

She shook her head. "No, you aren't." If she made a direct comparison of her ex-husband and Fisk, the balance would be way heavier on Fisk being a good guy. "You're all substance, not just looks. Although you have those." She reached over and pushed a shaggy strand of hair out of his eyes.

When she let her hand linger, he smiled, turned his head and kissed the palm of it.

Her heart pounded. She took deep breaths to calm down. "You're a good man. You help people, you love your family, you create beauty. Those are character qualities, good ones."

"Thank you," he said softly. "Your belief means the world to me, though I have more work to do on myself."

"Oh, so do I." She'd been thinking a little more counseling might be in order, just figuring out how to trust more and build a life in a totally different kind of community than she'd lived in before.

Although here, friends might serve as well as counselors. There was more potential for deep friendship here.

"So," he said, "a long engagement?"

She reeled back, staring at him. "What did you just say?"

A flush crossed his face. "I didn't mean to jump ahead, but I did, so…here goes. I already know I want to marry you. I won't expect you to—"

"Ask me," she demanded.

He knelt and Bonita clapped her hands, chortling up at Lauren.

Lauren blew the baby a kiss. And then she looked at Fisk's face and everything around her, including her child safe in Fisk's backpack, melted away.

"Will you…" he said, looking at Lauren. "And you…" He took hold of Bonita's leg. "Will you marry me?"

They were on the narrow berm of the road, caught in each other's eyes, and it was only Nemo's loud, persistent yapping that let them know a vehicle was approaching. As Fisk scrambled to his feet and wrapped protective arms around Lauren, pulling her farther off the road, a horn starting honking. And honking.

Gramps rode in the passenger seat of a classic car driven by a gray-haired woman. Gramps lowered his window, and Lauren saw that there were three more people in the back seat, a man and two women. Everyone waved and said hello.

Given what had been interrupted, the whole encounter felt surreal to Lauren. She was interacting with Gramps and his friends completely on autopilot.

Gramps laughed quietly. "I see my being out of the way was good for you two." He waved a hand toward the other passengers. "And you can see that I've picked up a gang of ne'er-do-wells while I was away."

There was general laughter.

"Was I right in thinking you were making some kind of proposal?" Gramps asked Fisk.

"Yes, I was."

One of the women in the back seat squealed.

"And what was her answer?"

"She hasn't answered."

The driver turned off the car, and for a moment, the

world was silent. And then she heard the song of a bird and the crunch of Fisk's feet on the snow as he came back toward her.

"Well?" Gramps said. "Are you going to marry him, or not?"

All eyes were on Lauren. What should she say? Should she trust her heart?

Nemo yipped, and Bonita chortled again and waved her arms, drawing attention away from Lauren for a crucial moment. She shot up a prayer. *Father, is this of You?*

She looked around, at Gramps and Bonita, the elders she knew a little already from church, and Fisk. Looked at the mountain laurels and fir trees, green against the snow. A deep sense of peace descended on her.

"The answer," she said, firm and certain, "is yes."

Fisk caught her up in his arms and swung her around, gently so as not to jostle Bonita too much, but the baby loved it. Gramps called out, "Hear, hear!" and his friends clapped and took pictures on their phones.

Lauren just took it all in. There, on the same mountain road where she'd first met Fisk, her life had just taken an unexpected and wonderful turn. She looked up at the blue winter sky and closed her eyes in thanks.

Epilogue

Despite their intention of having a long engagement, Fisk and Lauren were married in the spring.

Fisk was in a hurry to start their life together, but he didn't want to jeopardize their marriage by going too fast. He only suggested moving up the date after his AA sponsor and their pastor okayed the idea. He'd had more counseling, and she'd had some, too, and then they'd gone to their pastor for premarital counseling together.

Fisk still wouldn't have pushed it, except he realized that Lauren was as impatient as he was. They'd been working together and eating meals with Bonita and Gramps, shoveling snow together and attending the same adult Sunday school class. They didn't want to be apart.

Bonita was growing and learning, changing every day. Fisk didn't want to miss out on any phase of her childhood. He, of all people, treasured every moment with a child. He was hoping to be able to adopt Bonita one day, but regardless, he wanted to be part of her family as she grew up.

So here they were, having a May wedding in the city park in Holiday Point.

The weather had cooperated, producing a blue sky and blossoming trees and grass that was greening up nicely.

The rivers rushed to their merge point, fed by spring rains high in the mountains.

Bonita and Nemo came down the aisle together, Bonita preening and throwing flowers and Nemo carrying the rings in a pouch on his back. They were the hit of the wedding, until Lauren walked in, completely gorgeous in a simple white dress, holding the arm of a teary-eyed Gramps Tucker.

Fisk couldn't take his eyes off her. He couldn't believe that God had been so good as to give her to him, flawed as he was.

That was God, though.

The rest of the service was a happy blur.

The beauty of a wedding in Holiday Point was that everything was so close together. After exiting the church, they'd simply collected Bonita and Nemo and crossed the street to the park to begin their celebration as friends rained birdseed on them, blessing their union.

In their casual version of a receiving line, everyone checked in with them early at the reception. Fisk was stunned to glimpse, in the distance, a face he hadn't seen in years, but recognized in a heartbeat. Frank.

His brother.

But different.

A scar crossed his face, and he walked with a distinct limp. With him was a service dog.

"Come meet someone important." Fisk took Lauren's arm, and they hurried across the broad green lawn to where Frank stood, waiting.

Fisk gave him a bro hug, then a real hug. "Have you talked to the folks? Cam and Alec?"

"A little at a time. Today you're the focus. Introduce me to your bride."

So he did, and Lauren studied Frank with interest, and they talked a little while Frank's service dog and Nemo sized each other up.

When Frank met Bonita, he melted. Apparently, he had the same Wilkins gene as his brothers: he loved babies. He politely asked Lauren's permission, then picked Bonita up and bounced her in a meaty, tattooed arm while she played with his overgrown beard.

"Quite a tough dog you've got there," Frank commented when his attention could finally be diverted from Bonita to Nemo. "Named after a Disney movie?"

"I didn't name him," Fisk protested, laughing. "His puppy raiser was a huge Disney fan."

Nemo seemed to read Frank's attitude, and he wasn't having it. He sat bolt upright in front of Frank, letting out a steady series of yips until Frank relented and petted him.

It figured that Frank had the most macho service dog possible, a large rottweiler with a blocky body and massive head. Nemo barked at him, too, until the rottweiler put a large paw on Nemo's head. Nemo lay down instantly. Frank roared with laughter. "Pecking order established. Just like among the Wilkins men."

Cam and Alec and their wives drifted over and the wedding threatened to turn into a big old Wilkins reunion. But Lauren had invited some old friends and she floated among them, as well as their church friends, including everyone. Once the band set up in a cleared-out pavilion, Gramps Tucker was the first to dance, with a series of pleased-looking partners. Even Lauren's mother, a pretty sixty-something lady, had shown up with a silver-haired Frenchman in tow. Fisk was pretty sure the woman wouldn't be a huge part of their lives, but you never knew. It was good to keep doors open, and Lauren seemed willing to do it.

Fisk's parents looked great in new wedding clothes. Fisk, Cam and Alec had taken Dad shopping for a suit, and the women had taken Mom. They stayed sober for photos and a good half hour into the reception. After that, there was a little rowdiness, but Alec and Cam handled it. Fisk was off duty for this one day.

He put an arm around Lauren and looked at his family and friends, at his new daughter, playing with another little girl, at the river and the trees and the sky.

They were in their community and the sun was shining. Life was so, so good. "Do you know how much I love you?" he asked, propping his forehead against hers.

"Love you more."

He kissed her. Then kissed her again. "How long do we have to stay at the reception?"

"At least a little bit longer," she said, her fingers tracing the back of his neck as she embraced him.

They were having a simple honeymoon, staying in a rustic-but-luxurious chalet in the Great Smoky Mountains. Fisk had bought Lauren a day at a nearby fancy spa, just to pamper her. There was lots else to do, too, from hiking to fine dining to live country music.

But Fisk had a feeling they wouldn't get out much.

He put a hand on Nemo's head and kept his other arm around Lauren. Bonita was on Lauren's other side, walking well, keeping up.

Fisk looked at her, and for just a moment he saw Scarlett. She would have loved to walk and run and dance. Fisk didn't understand why she'd had to be taken from him.

There was so much he didn't understand. But he did understand that now was the time for love, and these were the people God had put into his life. He'd do his best to protect them, work for them, love them.

"I almost forgot." Lauren waved her bouquet, full of small purple and white flowers. "I have to throw this."

Fisk yelled for attention, and his sisters-in-law took up the cry, and soon all the single ladies stood in a group, from young teenagers to Mrs. Wittinger, who had to be eighty-five. They were all laughing and several were backing away, claiming they wouldn't accept the bouquet, that they'd toss it elsewhere if it came to them.

Lauren turned her back and tossed the bouquet over her shoulder.

"Short!" Cam and Alec yelled as it flew through the air.

Nemo knew how to play fetch with the best of them. He raced toward the bouquet, caught it in his mouth and turned to Fisk, his dark eyes seeming to laugh.

"Give it to somebody," Fisk urged, doubting the dog would understand. He waved a hand toward the laughing crowd of women.

Nemo trotted to Mrs. Wittinger and nudged her hand with the bouquet until she took it, her cheeks going pink.

"Mrs. Wittinger, huh?" Fisk ran fingers through Lauren's hair. "Is there something we don't know about her?"

"Well… I did see Gramps seek her out after church last week," Lauren told him, laughing. "Apparently he's off the mystery lady and onto new adventures."

"You don't mind? You were pretty set against your grandfather dating anybody."

She stood on tiptoes and kissed him. "When we're so happy," she murmured, "I want everyone else to be happy, too."

She was so pretty and so kind. So *everything*.

Around them, people sat at the picnic tables or stood in small clusters, eating and talking. Kids ran from the food tables to the playground, shouting. Bonita struggled to keep up, and two of the older kids stopped to wait for her, holding out their hands.

Fisk had never felt so blessed. He couldn't help it; he kissed Lauren again. And then he picked her up by the waist and swung her around, and they danced.

* * * * *

*If you enjoyed this K-9 Companions book,
be sure to look for* Guarding Her Christmas Secret
*by Jill Weatherholt, available December 2024,
wherever Love Inspired books are sold!*

*And look for Lee Tobin McClain's next
K-9 Companions book, also a part of her
Holiday Point series, coming February 2025!*

Dear Reader,

Thank you for making another visit to Holiday Point with me! Lauren and Fisk have both suffered in the past, which makes them understand each other. But they have to work to overcome their own emotional barriers and open themselves to each other. Like many of us, they try to do that work on their own, but it takes God's loving touch to bring them true healing.

Of course, there's another element to Fisk's healing journey: Nemo! Nemo, Fisk's service dog, is based on my own dog's best neighborhood friend. The real Nemo isn't a service dog, but he's beautiful and smart and perfectly trained. And he does bark a lot when he's excited! I really enjoyed modeling Fisk's dog on a real one. Check out my social media for pictures! Or join my newsletter for book news, giveaways and cute pet photos. I'd love to have you as a subscriber.

If you'd like to read an additional, free novella set in Holiday Point, just search Harlequin's online reads to find Cam and Jodi's story, *Nanny for the Summer. A Companion for Christmas, A Mother's Gift* and *A Companion for His Son* are also set in Holiday Point, and Frank's story is coming soon. All can be read as stand-alones, but it's even more fun to read them together!

Wishing you a wonderful holiday season filled with faith, family, friends and good books.

All my best,
Lee